Chaotic Rain

Tirico K. Bell

authorHOUSE·

AuthorHouse™
1663 Liberty Drive
Bloomington, IN 47403
www.authorhouse.com
Phone: 833-262-8899

Published by AuthorHouse 04/04/2023

ISBN: 979-8-8230-0502-9 (sc)
ISBN: 979-8-8230-0501-2 (e)

Print information available on the last page.

This book is printed on acid-free paper.

Prologue

In the lush and green forest, an energy portal consisting of purple flames, green lighting, orange ice, black wind, blue lava, light and dark energy appeared for a minute then vanished. An abnormal boy of ten years old and an odd appearance appeared. He had dark black hair, vantablack eyes, pale grayish skin, carnivorous teeth, and sharpened nails on his hands and feet. He wore a white tattered vest, a tattered black shirt, and black tattered shorts. On his back, there are six bone spikes sticking out. Each individual one is a foot long and six inches wide. The boy looks around and walks to a small clearing to find a man with a fruit cart. The man looks up startled, then sees the boy and asked with concern "Are you ok, boy?" The boy doesn't respond, instead lunges at him and slashes him in his right set of ribs going right through him with his left hand. Next, he grabs him proceeding to slam him to the ground. Finishing him off by biting into his head and eating part of it.

While eating the dead body, he hears wings flapping. There in the clearing stood 3 dragons. The first two were half the size of the third one. Both reaching 85 feet high and 80 feet long not including their tails. A red dragon with dark gray spikes and a dark colored membrane. A glowing blue with crystal like spikes and wings. And the last dragon was blood red with black spikes and black webbed wings. "We were looking for wyverns and all we find is an insect child." says the red dragon as goes to bite the boy, who jumps in the air. "Scorch how could you miss?" The blue dragon said then proceeds to spray a beam of ice at the boy. While still in the air manages to dodge. "You missed too Hydra." Scorch says as he looks at Hydra. Both dragons now try to attack him together. For the next 20 minutes the fight has been the same. They attack and miss, while the boy claws off their scales.

Scorch finally manages to tackle the boy pinning him down. However, is quickly impaled in his knuckle by the child. "Aah!!" screams Scorch. "You two leave and tell the other dragons about this thing." "Yes, Blood fang." said both dragons. As both begin to fly off, Scorch is then attacked, the boy proceeds to dig inside of him." Aah! Aah!" Blood fang looks in shock as Scorch stops screaming and dies. Hydra continues to fly off to warn the other dragons. Something emerges from the body. A dragon creature the same size as Blood fang. It looks at Blood fang and lets out a combination of a roar and a screech. Both then throw themselves at each other. Blood fang bites into the shoulder of the creature. In turn it bites his wing. The dragon starts to claw at the beast knocking him off. The dark monster decides to stab him in the arm with his tail.

Chapter 1

After a week of flying Hydra finally sees the mountain up ahead. Now he can tell the others what has transpired. After landing on the obsidian and crystal ground, he enters the cave. Inside the massive cave there are many large tunnels, with all types of minerals. Plenty of them like gold, silver, titanium, steel, diamond and crystal. Hydra walks deeper and sees a group of dragons further in. Three dragons in total, two which is the same size as him. While the last one was the same size as Blood fang. Acid yellow scales covered her body. A purplish pink underbelly with a membrane of the same color. Dark green spikes lay on the back. Teeth and claws were the same shade of green. Greenish blue spots were spread out on the yellow scales. Her tail has a thorn shaped tip. That is how one of the smaller ones looked.

The other smaller dragon had midnight blue scales. Blueish gray patterns adored certain spots of her body. Standing out on the blue scales. Dull gray claws protruded from her hands. Short gray horns stood at the back of her head.

Finally, the larger dragon had obsidian scales. His wings were bulky with gems of different colors sticking out. He had an underbelly of crystal. Quart spines spread across his back. Crystal spikes covered his arms, and his claws were made of diamond.

Moving closer he says "Calamity, Viper, Mist, we have a situation!" He says urgently. The yellow dragon stares at him with her azure pupil and scarlet sclera eyes. "What situation? Where is Scorch and Blood fang?" "We were looking for wyverns, however, didn't find any." Hydra says. "Then we ran into what we thought was a deformed human child. Scorch and I proceeded to try and kill the child. Thinking it was going to be easy." Hydra narrows his eyes and continues. "However, that was not the case. Every attack we threw at it was dodged."

Hydra looks at his wounds that have partial healed. Feeling mildly ashamed. "Then it retaliated, slowly it was slashing our scales off with its claws. The pain wasn't that bad, but the fact the creature could do it was worrying. So, Blood fang told us to go warn the others and he would deal with the thing. As me and Scorch was flying, it jumped into the air and grabbed Scorch, bringing him to the ground." All three of them looked at me in shock. Hydra continues to tell them about what happened. "That's when it started to dig and burrowed inside of him. Scorch screams stopped and the abomination emerged from his corpse. However, it's form was different, now it looked like us dragons. That's when I finally left to warn y'all and the others."

Mist speaks up, barely believing what she has heard. "Do you know if Blood fang is alive?" Viper then pops in and says, "Of course he is alive, I doubt he died to this creature, if this story is true." Hydra looks at her. "I am telling the truth. I don't know if Blood fang is dead or not. The trip from there to here is about a week." The obsidian dragon Calamity finally says something. "Well, us four can go and see what the situation is. If it is bad, then we return to tell the rest of our group what has happen." The younger dragons seeing no problem with this nod and exits the cave with him. They all start flying to where the fight happened.

Hours after Hydra left, Blood fang's battle continues. They have transitioned the fight into the sky, both opponents are injured. Blood fang sprays a magma beam at the beast, who in turns fires a black laser. Both attacks hit head on and looked equal but then the laser shoots through the beam and hits the left half of Blood fang. He falls to the ground almost dead. The dark beast lands on top of him and bites his neck finishing him. After consuming part of the flesh, the creature starts having pieces of himself falling off. As they hit the ground their forms start to take shape.

The forms that are taken on, are humanoid. However, unlike the boys first form, these creatures don't look human in the slightest. They have bone white skin, black claws and razor teeth, light gray scales and small spikes on their heads. Then the creatures, they all look up at the first creature. The creature looks around and sees humans that have witnessed the fight. "Kill all the humans here and drag the most you can from the bodies." The creatures lunge toward the humans who start to scream. "Aah!" Many people shrieked as they are torn apart. With all the people dead, the creatures start to dismember the bodies to drag away. Some of the creatures proceed to take pieces of the dragons off. "Let's go." The monster walks in a direction with the creatures following him.

The group of dragons finally arrive to the clearing. "This is where we engaged the creature." Hydra commented. They look around the area and spot the decomposing remains of Scorch and Blood fang. *"So, that is what remains of them."* He thought sadly. All that was left was the rotting right side of Scorch's upper torso with his head. There was more left of Blood fang's corpse, but he was missing his limbs and part of his left shoulder. "Dang! They are dead! You were telling the truth!" Viper exclaims. *"This creature must be powerful. It took out Scorch and Blood fang!"* Viper thought in shock. The faces of the dragons so their displeasure. Landing on the ground, the bodies are examined. Calamity moves to look at Blood fang.

"That confirms what you told us Hydra. It also seems Blood fang is dead." Hydra moves closer to Blood fang's body and sees bite marks on his neck. Looking further over the body, he notices parts of charred flesh on the left side. "It seems he was burnt on his left side and the finishing blow was a bite to the neck." Hydra replies. "What creature can fight two dragons and win?" said Viper. Her and Mist near Scorch's remains. Mist speaks up. "We should check the area for it. Maybe it died further away after the fight." *"Hopefully we won't have a problem on our hands."* Thought Mist pleading.

They all look at her and nod. "That is a reasonable thing to do. Plus, we are going to have to look for it anyway to handle the threat if it is alive." Calamity tells them. *"Can't believe you are dead my old friend."* He thought sadly. Proceeding to walk forward, following any traces it could have left and the rest follow. Walking for a while, they find themselves upon a human village. Or at least what remains of one. They continue into the village, looking around and seeing rotting limbs, destroyed buildings. "It seems the creature has been through here." Viper concludes. *"Wonder why it would come through here for?"* Viper confusedly thought. "At least this shows we are on the right track." Replies Mist. "Looks like it has killed all the humans here. Let's move forward." Pushing forward the dragons leave the village.

"Looks like it went on a war path." Mist couldn't help but think this. *"What was it's reasoning to do all this?"* Hydra was at a loss. It just didn't make sense to him.

Now arriving at the forest of this region. They all look around seeing that something has indeed happened here. "What has happened here. Many trees look like they been knocked down." Mist says while looking at the broken trees. Her companions having nothing to say about this. Walking further in, they see remains of animals. "Looks like something has killed the animals here. It may be what we are hunting for." Calamity spoke, as they witness pieces of animals and random areas covered in blood. *"So far it only leaves destruction in its wake."* Calamity states in his head.

Continuing onward in the forest, more blood and small pieces of animals are seen. "It really did a number on this place. Look at all this dried blood here." Viper says looking in bewilderment. "There even seems to be parts from trolls here." States Hydra, who is looking at different parts of trolls spiraled around. There are large spots of dry blood on the trees and rocks. "Do you think it was trying to show dominance? Possible even marking its territory?" Mist wonders out loud. "This is just a massacre and nothing else." Calamity says. They continue looking around the forest for traces of the creature. However, they just see limbs and dried blood. *"Yeah, I think this could only be a massacre."* Hydra saw no other way. "Especially when there is no pattern. It's just killing." Hydra adds his input.

After an hour of searching and finding nothing, they figure it's time to go. "It's time we go back and go warn the others. We are not going to find anything, and we need everyone prepared." Calamity tells them. "This threat might bigger than thought."

Hydra nods "I agree. Without any traces or clues to find it would be pointless otherwise." *"Plus, this allows us to think of how to break the information to the clan."* He supportably thought. Flying in the air the flock of dragons leave the area. With one objective, warn the others as they go home. Leaving the forest behind, we see as they fly in the distance.

"How exactly are going to explain, what has happened to the rest of our flock?" Viper curiously asked. *"It is not like we can just say it."* She thought. Even she thought what has happened outlandish.

Viper turns and looks at Calamity, wondering how they are going to go about this. The other two look at as well. This is an important question.

Calamity looks at them in thought. *"That is a good question. However, it is not hard to answer."* Nodding his head at them. "Will tell them step by step, detail by detail. Starting with your mission and what transpired. Then we tell them about our search."

"That makes sense. Ok. So, I tell them what me and my team were doing. Then about the creature." Replied Hydra. *"That way we cover all our bases. Especially with the disbelief of their deaths and the reaction to this monster."* Hydra analyzing the plan in his mind.

They all focus back to flying back to their home. Which is going be a lengthy trip.

In another location conflict is high. There is a large village of humans running about. Fire cackling everywhere you look. Buildings made of clay, brick and wood. Pathways leading from the inside of the village to the outside. Horses and cows running about terrified. Wagons all over the place rather in good shape or destroyed. Farms ruined and on flames.

Blood on everything in sight. Even on the people running around screaming. "Aah! Aah! Someone help?! Please help me?!" Shouts a woman trying to run. She is covered in blood.

"How can something like this happen!" She terrifically thought. "Somebody! Please save me! Save mee-!" She is interrupted by a pale white creature with black spikes tackling her. It starts clawing at her. Then takes a bite out her neck. **Rip! Tear!** Blood spurting out of the wound like a fountain.

There more of these creatures running about. They are chasing the humans, horses, and cows. One tackles a horse and bites down on its neck. **Crack! Crunch!** It starts feasting on the horse.

A bunch of the creatures are swarming the town. Some breaking into buildings and killing the people inside. Others going around killing the cows. They were killing everything in sight.

A large cluster of them are racing towards the center of the village. There plenty of dead knights on the ground this path. Soon we start seeing bloodied and wounded knights fighting.

"Aah! We can't hold!" A knight says before being grabbed and ripped apart. Another knight swings his sword and kills one of the creatures.

"Why is there so many!" He screams. Trying to kill another one but misses. Not too long 3 of them jump on him killing him.

"No! I don't want to die!" Are the last words of a knight.

The remaining knights are in a tight circle. The buildings around them are broken. Roofs caved in and even covered with the monsters. All around the knights are dead bodies of the beasts and of humans.

They currently are surrounded by the things. Each one circling the knights.

"Why did this happen?" One knight wondered in fear. He swings and cuts one of the monsters. More of the knights started swinging too. "We must hold them back! Then we can kill them." He sternly says.

After he says that another knight is grabbed and was torn apart. Screams filling the night as more knights were killed.

"What are these things! They keep coming in mass." Another knight stated. As more got closer, they were shot by a cannon. **Boom!** Cannon still smoking maned by a random man.

"What is this guy thinking!" The knight thought incuriously. The man looks down at them. "Don't worry I got your backs!" He yells as he tries to run toward another cannon. He is however cut short of doing that. One of the creatures leaped at him.

"Aah! Aah! Aah!" His blood curdles screams end as the monster rips out his throat with its teeth. "No! We lost our only support!" One of the knights' shouts.

All the beasts charge the knights. "Aah!" The knights' shout as they charge. The knights give it their all but was for naught. They barely manage to kill any of the beasts.

"We weren't going to survive this. We never stood a chance." One of them sourly thought. One by one the knights start to die off. Eventually they are all ripped apart by the creatures. Which all but rush to consume their meal.

Chapter 2

A blue creature is slammed into the ground. As it tries to struggle, it's throat is ripped out. The assailant is a young dragon. Coal black scales with razor blade spikes and ash gray claws. The wings have razor hooks on them and is partly translucent. Getting up from its kill, looks to see another of the blue creatures. Almost the same size as him, with armor like skin with metallic fur. *"Only a few raijus left."* The dragon says to himself in his mind. *"They were a little bit of a challenge. I admit that much."*

Rolling into an armor ball the raiju charges at him covered in electricity. Surprisingly he does the same, but it is a spike ball. They clash and the raiju is slammed back. Both unroll and start slashing at each other.

Electric claws slice into scales and slightly burn flesh. "Argh!" The dragon growls a little in pain and swipes at the raiju. However, the claws only scratch the skin, but he quickly follows up with stabbing at it. **Hiss!** Once he impaled it starts swinging it with his razor tail. Being tossed a little away, it shoots a beam of electricity at the dragon. **Crackling! Sizz!** Though the attack only grazes him because he partly dodged.

"All right! I am done with this! Just die!" The coal black dragon thought angrily. Sick of these games. *"This fight is over!"*

Getting fed up with this fight, he retaliates with his own beam. The beam is made of slime like blades. The raiju attempts to dodge but is hit in the leg crippling it. Flesh of the leg is filled with the blades and part of it is missing.

"Aah! Mewl!" The pain makes the raiju screech. Then it starts to whimper in pain.

Trying to flee, it is stopped. "Where do you think are you going?" Says the dragon and proceeds to stab the raiju in the neck with the blades on his wrist. *"It really thought it could escape. Well, that is another dead. Wonder how the others are doing."* The dragon wondered to himself.

Proceeding to look around past all the raiju bodies, he spots what is looking for. Looking at a young dark gray dragon with titanium spikes. "Aqua how are you holding up?" Aqua kills a raiju by extending a few of her spikes into it. "Doing quite well actually. I see you finished killing the ones over there, Vein." She speaks. *"Guess there none left over here."* Aqua concludes in her mind.

"Yeah, the last one put up more of a fight than the others. Do you know where Scourge is at?" *"Hopefully that is all of them. If so, Scourge will probably tell us it's time to leave."* He thought in hope and relief.

Before she can respond, a raiju starts running towards them. Only making it a few feet from them, it is crushed into the ground by a full-grown dragon. Seeing the raiju in the dragon's claws was like seeing a rat in the talons of an owl.

A flesh red dragon with tendril like wings, speaks to them. "I see y'all have gotten everything taken care over here. This is the last raiju in the region." Finishing her sentence, she proceeds to use her wing tendrils to impale its head. "All the ones we didn't kill ran off. That however is ok, they know better to try to claim this territory now." *"They did well on their part."* She thought proud of them both.

"Yes! What is the next mission Scourge?" "For now, we are returning to Minera mountain. That way we can see what the others are up to and plan the next mission after rest." She answers Aqua and then informs them of their next action. *"That makes sense. We got to report the success of our mission first to continue to another assignment. Plus, we might not have another task any way."* Aqua thought in realization.

Scourge, Vein, and Aqua take off into the air. Each carrying and eating a raiju corpse. *"Got to admit raijus taste good."* Vein thought enjoying his meal. After flying out of the region, they see something odd unfolding. Looking down they see a small skirmish happening. A group of owlbears are fighting bone white boar like creatures with dark grey spikes. *"Huh? What are those creatures fighting the owlbears?"* Aqua thought to herself.

"Do either one of you know what those white and black creatures are?" Vein asks both Scourge and Aqua.

"Nope never seen these beasts before." Aqua replies with just as much confusion as Vein. "What about you Scourge? Have you ever encountered these creatures before?"

Scourge shakes her head. "No, I have never encountered anything like this. Not once in my long life." She tells them. "Though it is impressive that they can handle owlbears."

Even though they are three times the size of the boar creatures, they have taken more losses. Five owlbears are dead while only two of the beasts are dead. An owlbear uses its crystal talons to slash at one of the beasts. It is sent flying, then it covers its feathers in crystal. Another boar goes to attack the much larger creature and trying to bite its neck. However, it is stabbed by the talons of the owlbear. **Swoosh!** Another boar is taking out by a crystal feather thrown at it.

Its victory is however short lived. 2 of the creatures tackle it to the ground. **Rip! Tear! Splash!** Soon its throat is ripped out and the creatures it goes towards another owlbear. It only had time to throw a feather at one of them. **Scree!** The feather hit and skewered the boar. The other white and gray creature pounces onto the owlbear. It is killed shortly after.

Soon the remaining owlbears are killed with barely any resistance. "Huh? That was weird." Vein concludes. *"They handled the owlbears without much effort. They had numbers too, but not that much."* Thought to himself.

"Didn't think that would happen." Aqua responds. *"At first glance it looked like the owlbears would win."* She could not help but think. Scourge turns to them. "I will admit, I am too shocked that the owlbears lost. Those creatures are indeed impressive."

The three continued on their way back home. Flying over a few more regions and environments, they only left to go. After a week and a half, they have arrived back to the mountain. *"Oh! Finally, we are back. I can relax now."* Aqua thought in happiness.

"What do you think the others are up to?" Vein asked them both curious. *"It has been a while since we have seen the others. Wonder if they completed their missions. Some probably failed theirs."* Vein thought this humorously.

"Really, I not sure what they might be up to. Don't forget that everyone may not be back." Scourge responded to his question. "After we inform the rest of the clan of the success of the mission. Can we rest for a bit? You know regain our energy." Aqua asked Scourge with hope in her tone.

"Yes. You both can get some rest once we update our status. So, make sure to get all you can." She informs them both. She can practically feel the joy exploding from Aqua. Walking into one of the entrances, prepare to report their mission. Unaware of what news they are about to learn.

There are three dragons fighting hundreds of trolls. There is a strong hold that the trolls live in. A gray dragon swipes at the trolls and kills many. The trolls swing all sort of weapons at a young purple dragon. Only for them to bounce off its scales. Opening its mouth and releasing a ray of poisonous gas.

The poison eats through their leather armor. "Argh! Aah! Aah! Argh!" Screams of trolls feel the surrounding area. In the distance near the stronghold is a stone dragon hitting with a beam of stone.

"You puny trolls think those insignificant weapons can hurt us! Die for your insolence." The gray one menacingly tells them. *"How dare they challenge us. They will pay for their mistake with their lives."* He angrily thinks. Next, he sprays them with burning ash. The ash burns through the armor and starts killing them.

"Aah! Aah! It burns!" They scream and shout in their language. **Thud! Thud! Thud!** Many bodies fall and hit the ground. He looks at all the bodies in disgust. *"Absolutely revolting. I hope we will be done soon."* He hopes so they can leave.

Turning to where the purple dragon was. "Roy! Are you almost done!? I am done with these trolls." He says with snark in his voice. "Almost got them over here, Jim. Don't be in such a rush." Roy replies to him teasingly.

"Here he goes again with his shenanigans. I hate it we he does that." He thought annoyed. "Just hurry up! That way we can help Tom and be done."

"Slow your roll. Plus, I think he is done anyway. He will most likely tell us to search the perimeter to make sure they are all dead." Roy shot back at him.

Flap! Flap! The sound of wings flapping catches their attention. "Ah, you both are finished here." Tom says to them both. "I finished on my end. With that done, all of us are going to check the surroundings. Can't let there be any stragglers." He tells them with a dead serious voice.

"So, once we do finish clearing the area, we will be returning. I like that." Jim states tiredly.

All of them went to check different spots in the area. Jim found three trolls trying to hide. After scoffing at them he ends their lives with burning ash. Roy saw some half dead ones trying to crawl away. Laughing at their misfortune, finding them struggling amusing. He goes ahead and crushes them under his claws.

Tom was looking around and spotted some trolls trying to run. He catches up to them very easily. They tried to attack him with their puny weapons. All Tom did was move his tail, then smashed them with it.

"Alright, we are done here. Now we return to the mountain." After Tom said that they all took to the air. Flying further out they see razorbacks. Large boar sloth like creatures with porcupine quills. They seem to be fighting other group of creatures.

The creature fighting them are small. They are feline like creatures with white skin and black back spikes. The razorbacks use their claws to slash the creatures.

While getting rid of some. It ultimately did nothing. The creatures are then hit with quills. Impaling multiple ones, but that doesn't stop them.

Soon they just overwhelmed the razorbacks. Taking them out one by one. The last of the beast are killed by the strange creatures.

The dragons continuing flying on their way. All wondering what those creatures were.

A week has passed after they checked the location of Blood fang and Scorch's bodies. The four dragons are getting ready to tell the others here what has happened. Looking at the gathering dragons here, while there are still a few teams on missions, they are ready to warn them. As Hydra is about to speak, three dragons walk in. "Hey, what is happening here? Are we having a gathering?" Vein asked. Wondering why everyone here is gathered.

"Yes, we have terrible news. Not only is Blood fang and Scorch dead, but a new creature did it and it is a threat." Hydra tells all the dragons of the hunt and death of their follow dragons.

"Then he came here and told us what happened." Calamity states. "So, we went with him to validate his claims. We arrived at the location and saw the remains. Half of Scorch was missing, and chunks was taken from Blood fang. Not only that but Blood fang had burn marks." Scourge replies. "Whatever the creature used must be hot and strong to burn Blood fang. Not only is it pretty much unheard to burn a magma dragon. Blood fang is literally the strongest magma dragon." "Yes, I was of the same thought process." Calamity agrees.

Viper continues the tale. "After that we started to try and track the creature. We arrived at a human village that has been clearly attacked. There were body parts all over and buildings destroyed. So, all of us continued until we reached the forest." She finishes. "Something clearly had happened in the forest. Searching in the forest, show all types of remains such as animals and trolls." Mist ends the tale. Hydra tells that is when they came to warn the others.

"Wait a minute. Are those white creatures that killed the owlbears part of this?" Vein thought questionably. "I don't know if this is connected, but we saw creatures with similar colors." Vein explains with hesitation. He informs them of what they saw while they were flying. "Do you think these creatures are like the beast? Or a cause of concern?" *"The description sounds similar."* Vein thought about it. Looking at Hydra and the others to see if this a piece of the puzzle.

"While the description is canny, I can't put them together." Hydra thought it over. "I am not sure. This could be two different cases." Hydra worriedly replies. *"Now that I remember. Those feline things had the same colors."* Tom thought about. "No. I believe it is connected." Looking at the stone dragon that spoke up. "What makes you so sure?" "The reason is because I saw Feline like creatures with the same colors and spikes. They were barely bigger than wolves, yet a few took out a group of razorbacks."

"That is concerning. We should investigate different areas and regions. That way we can see if this happening anywhere else." Calamity firmly says, as he ponders the connections. *"If there is more of the creature that will be a problem. For all we know it could be its offspring which is just as bad."* He thought worriedly.

"We should leave in three groups each. This will allow us to better prepare if worse comes to pass." Words wisely spoken by Scourge. The dragons leave in their groups, to find any similar events.

I look at Scourge, Calamity, and Lance, as we fly in the air. Seeing how I did not have a group anymore; I was told to go with them. *"I wouldn't be in this situation if that monster didn't kill my team! It is all that vile creature's fault!"* Hydra thought bitterly. Mist looks over at Hydra. *"It must be tough not having a team anymore. I guess from now on he will either be on Calamity's or Scourge's team."* She thought feeling bad for Hydra.

All of us have been looking for any sign of these creatures in two different regions. However there hasn't been any spotted. Though that looks like that might change today. "Hey, what is happening down there?" Viper asked curiously. Looking down we see a battle taking place.

The battle is between two species. One of which is the hikoyasei, bat creatures averagely the size of adolescent dragons. Fur and skin are normally gray, brown, or orange. Boar and bear like creatures with bone white skin and black spikes. And lending the creatures is a young humanoid girl with ashen white skin. Gray shoulder hair, neutral gray eyes, black claws and 2-inch spikes from her back.

"Let's see how this plays out. Then engage if necessary." Lance says strategically. We all nod and move closer to see the fight. *"All I know is I am started to believe that these things are indeed connected to that creature. And all of them will die the same."* I think angrily. *"Blood fang and Scorch will be avenged."*

Chapter 3

"I can just fill the rush of pleasure from just killing these creatures." I thought blissfully. Looking around at the dark quills, that I lead here to fight for our apex White spine. After we pushed the hikoyasei colony out of the mountain, the fun began. **Shoo! Slick! Tear! Rip!** Slashing an orange one and ripping it's arm off, then I killed it. A hikoyasei pins down a dark quill with acid silk, before biting off its head. Multiple of the bats are then swarmed and taken from the air. Killing and eating their flesh, the dark quills get bigger and develop wings.

Now that some of the dark quills can fly, they start to fight in the air. "Yes! Go forth and kill them all! Take their DNA for White spine!" I yell to my fellow dark quills. *"These hikoyasei won't be able beat us."* I confidently think to myself.

Rip! Tear! I run forward and grab a gray hikoyasei, then start to rip it apart. Jumping in the air to dodge a glob of acid silk. Then I grab the brown bat, slamming it to the ground. **Boom! Tear!** Next, I rip its jaws off. "They are foolish to think they stand a chance. None of them can stop me!" I thought laughing to myself. As I get ready to kill more of these bats, I am grabbed and thrown to a secluded area.

Thud! Crack! I hit the ground roughly. I catch my bearings and start to get up. As I look up in the sky, I see five larger hikoyasei. *"Huh? Is that what grabbed me? They look different from the others. Not only are they bigger. They have different colors from the rest."* She thought to herself confused.

Two of them are thrice the size of the normal ones. The other three are only double the size. The smaller three have bright colors. One has blue skin and dark blue fur. Another has red skin and crimson fur. The last of the three has green skin and mosslike fur. The larger two contrast each other, one is snow white. While the other one is pitch black.

"Do they believe they can beat me? Hah! Ridiculous." I thought humorously. I already know that I will win. "This will be easy! You can't win!" I say arrogantly. Running forward and lunging at the green one. I miss, as it dodges and the red one sprays red acid at me. "Aah!" It burns through my skin and almost removes my arm. **Sizzle! Fizz!** The acid melting my skin fazes out. Just as my skin and flesh start to heal, I am grabbed. **Stab! Crush!** "Augh!" *"Ah! That kind of hurts. This won't last long."* I reassure in my mind. Feeling the talons of the green one piercing my body, straight through. **Crash!** Getting tossed into a tree. Almost instantly, my body is crushed into the ground. Following up, by being flung into the air, just for red to skydive me. And then to be slammed into floor.

"All right! I have had enough of these bats! They don't know who they are messing with!" I thought in my mind, beyond angry. **Crack! Pop! Snap! Squelch!** The sound of a body popping fills the area.

Feeling my bones slowly fix themselves, I stand. "ENOUGH! You all will pay for this!" Pissed that they have been whooping my ass for 20 minutes. *"It's time for them to die. Let's see them handle my other form."* I bitterly and angrily ponder. I began to transform and take off into the air. The red one tries to tackle me out the air. However, I grab him with my talons. I may be a third smaller, but this makes him easier to hit. Using my razor bug like wings, proceeds to start cutting up the bat.

"Do you like that?! Huh! This is what happens when you miss with me!" I start to taunt and laugh. "Ahh! Ahh!" As it shrieks in pain, I capitalize while it is distracted. My razor wing decapitates it.

Letting its body fall below, I move my body out of the way of a stream of acid. **Swoosh! Hiss!** *"Did this hikoyasei, just try to sneak attack me, really? How dare it! It must pay!"* Looking at green and returning the favor. Green is hit by my ash white laser and is burned. Slamming into it. I start biting it with my mandibles. It starts flaring about as, while I start to eat it. "Aah! Aah! Ah**!" Crunch! Snap! Drip!** Its whining fades as I eat its shoulder and chest. Tossing the corpse to the ground, getting bigger.

Crack! Snap! Pop! My bug like wings snap and transform into batlike ones. I fly towards blue with my now batlike wings. *"You won't even last with me in this form. You will be ripped to shreds!"* Me knowing its fate is seal couldn't help but thought humorously.

"Prepare to join your friends, vermin! Know the stupidity in challenging us. Everyone last one of you will be torn apart." Clawing at the blue one, it retaliates by biting my shoulder. Tussling in the sky, I throw blue off me. Claws brandished ready to cut is stopped by blue acid. My claws burned off from the counter.

"Aah! You vermin! You will suffee-!" I am slammed into, and its teeth start digging into my head. *"How is this vermin individual keeping up with me?! This will not stand!"* I start clawing at the attacker and prying the jaws off me.

Keeping the mouth open, releases the ash white laser down its throat. The lifeless body falls to the land. **Thud!** The dark quill growls at the two last hikoyasei. *"I am sick of all these wretched creatures. I am ending these."*

As she lunges toward them, she is intercepted by a blast of ice. Huffing in pain, she turns to see where that attack from. "What the!" Only for a gray dragon to ram into her. Scourge and the others are beaming the dark quills from the air. Hydra and Lance come to help the gray dragon.

A group hikoyasei jump and kill an orange dragon. The others retaliate and kill those hikoyasei. The black bat releases a shrill and flies off with the white one. Soon all other hikoyasei start flying behind them and leave. "I guess we don't have worry about the hikoyasei anymore." Vein said to the others. "Good! Getting mobbed by them would be annoying and dangerous." Viper says back.

The gray dragon is bisected before anyone can reach him. "You foul creature! How dare you kill him?!" Lance yells in rage. Releasing a stream of rock at the dark quill. Barely dodging she calls for help. "Dark quills distract them! We must report this!" *"Why are dragons here!"* She thought in terror.

The dark quills rush at Hydra and Lance stalling them. While a few leave with their leader. "No come back and die!" *"How dare that wretched beast kill my disciple!"* He thinks in fury. His thoughts end once he is swarmed. The stone dragon is completely covered, and his wings destroyed. Once he falls to the ground, he is rip apart. "We must exterminate these things. Or will get mobbed." One of Vein's forelegs morphs into a tube shape with hooks. "I agree." One of Aqua's arms change shape to with spikes sticking out.

Rapidly firing projectiles into the swarm. **Boom! Boom! Boom! Boom! Boom! Boom!** The dark quills are ravaged by 1,000 to 2,000 projectiles per minute. Dark quills that are not being fired on, are blasted by elements from the other dragons. The surrounding trees are destroyed. The ground and other surrounding area cracked.

Three of the beasts try to take out Hydra. However, he reacts quickly by forming blades of ice. Swinging his arms towards them, severs their heads.

"Alright that is all of them. They weren't too hard." *"I was kind of expecting more."* Viper thought underwhelmed. "You can say that again. The only thing going for them were numbers. Hey, Hydra was the one that got away like the creature that killed Blood fang and Scorch?" Aqua states to Viper and then asked Hydra.

"Yes, it did almost the same thing that the monster did. Only difference was the reversed colors. And how it transformed before absorbing their powers. Also, when it did absorb one of them, it added part of its traits. Rather than becoming one of them with its own colors. These creatures are definitely; linked to each other."

"Then we need to head back and tell the others about the situation. Maybe even find out if anything happened on their end. All that is known for certain is we must exterminate these dark quills." Calamity states with a bit of edge in his voice.

"Let's go ahead and pick up their bodies, so we can leave." Scourge says dispassionately. Moving she picks up the orange dragon's body. Once the other bodies are picked up, they take off into the sky. Mist looks back at the bodies of the dark quills.

"Do you all think we will be able to kill them all?" Mist asked out loud. "If they are as weak as this, then it will be as easy as slicing through a glit wing. They will be too weak to do anything to us. It will just be moths to a flame." Viper arrogantly replies.

"I would be careful of what you say Viper. Let's not forget one of them is as strong as us. There might be more on that level." Aqua warily spoke. *"It would be bad if we were swarmed by ones of that level. I don't know if we could handle that."* She worriedly thinks.

Vein quickly adds, "Plus those cannon fodder can be a distraction for the stronger ones. Also, if you are swarmed by them, you can still die. Look at what happened to Lance." *"That is not a way I want to go out. Wings broken then falling and crashing into the ground just to be ripped apart. That was just awful."* Vein thinks with a shiver.

They all continue their journey back. Wondering what plans are going to need action. One thing on their minds, which was how will this play out.

"It is sad that Lance died. Not only that his apprentices died too. First Blood fang and Scorch, and now Lance and his apprentices. These new creatures have killed too many dragons already! They must be stopped!" Thought Calamity remorsefully for his deceased friends.

"Now that I know these dark quills are connected to that creature. I will do everything in my power to kill every single one of them. All the way to that abomination." Hydra thought with rage and revenge in his heart. He will murder every, last one.

Scourge turns and looks at Hydra. *"Hopefully he won't let this get to him. Revenge can lead people to death if not harnessed probably. Hopefully we won't lose any more people."* She can only think hopefully.

Chapter 4

Six goliaths are standing in a sandy clearing. All having toad like skin with spikes. Short tails following behind them. 2 of the 6 is the size of adult dragons. The other 4 are the size of adolescent ones. Clancy the obsidian goliath is in deep thought. *"This generation of goliaths look promising. Especially mine and Spin ray's group."* Looking at the smaller goliaths with pride in his heart.

He has grayish obsidian skin. Cyan colored stripes went across his body. His spikes emerged from his back and made of crystal.

"Listen up youngsters! We are going hunting and you 4 will be evaluated on how well you did." Spin-ray the cactus adult instructs. She is a purplish brown with hints of pink. Cactus fins rest on her back. On her arms are thorn like spikes. On display above her head is a pair of vine like antlers.

Solar a indigo goliath youngster, looks up with a grin. "We got this hunt handled. Nothing is taking us down." His head is spear shaped. There were a few purple spikes across his body.

"Don't get ahead of yourself Solar. We still need to see what prey, we are after. That way we can plan." Dawn playfully informs. The wood like one looks at the rock goliath. "Don't you agree Chloe?" "Yes, I agree." She replies stoically. Von a grey colored goliath just looked at them plainly.

Dawn is a deep brown with her having wooden exoskeleton. Her underbelly is an undertone of gray. Wooden spikes decorated her body. Chloe was a desert orange color. With a rocky shell covering her body. Four horns pointing outward and spikes on her tail. As for Von. He has small spikes over his frame. His head was also shark like.

"Now remember only you 4 are doing the hunting. We will be watching and will not intervene." Clancy looks Spin-ray. "Let's go ahead and take them to their targets." "Yes, they all look ready." Clancy and Spin ray leads the rest to the location.

The group travels through the desert. All around are tree sized cacti and metallic mangru trees. In the distance there is random diamond like bushes. Glistening in the horizon is random lakes and ponds.

"Traveling through the land is wonderful. I get see it and all its beauty." Chole happily thought. Looking around at all flora and vibrant colors. Glancing at the others to see what they are up to. She sees Dawn moving her short tail in the air.

Arriving in a field of cacti, that are blue and red. In the field eating the cacti are a group of whale-sized land fish. *"I wonder if this is what we are going to hunt."* Solar wondered to himself. He turned to look at Spin-ray and Clancy.

"These are the targets you will have to hunt. Each one of you must kill a sand skipper." *"Let's see how they do."* When the 4 left to start the hunt, she turns to Clancy. "How well do you think they will do?" "I believe the four of them will succeed. The question is what methods they will use." *"I do wonder what methods they will use."*

"I have to carefully approach the sand skipper." Von crawls silently towards one using a cactus as cover. Once in range he jumps onto his prey. Opening his mouth wide, his jaw splitting in half. Releasing a ball of white acid on its head. After seeing it die, looks at the other three.

Solar is clawing at a sand skipper's throat. Chloe was biting out the neck of another. While Dawn had impaled the one, she had in the head. The rest of the sand skippers open their mouths and start screaming. Next, they flee, some digging into the ground and leaving.

"Well looks we all got one. Wasn't too hard." *"I wonder how we are going to be graded."* Dawn curiously wonders. All the young goliaths look at the adults walking toward them. "You all have done well. With the hunt complete, you may eat your kill." After hearing his words, they start to feast.

While Solar and others are enjoying their kills, Clancy starts thinking how they did. *"I knew they would succeed. They also did with such efficiency."* Looking around at the smaller ones. *"They will most likely get far in life."* "After y'all are finish eating, we will go to 1 of the lakes. You will drink from it and be told how well you did."

Once they are finished eating, they set out. Arriving at the closest lake.

Near the lake is a group of moth rays. They are a cousin species to the goliaths. Large newt like creatures with claws, normally having spikes or fins. There seems to be a scuffle between them and bug like creatures. They seem to be pale white with black spikes.

One of them is crushed in the hand of a moth ray. A moth ray shoots out its barbed bladed tongue into the bug. Opening its mouth, top jaw splitting in half, reels it in. After eating it, they turn around.

"Oh, a group of moth rays. Hope they don't try to start something." All of them start growling in their language. "Calm yourselves. We are not here to kill you." Clancy calmly states. They continue their growling but do nothing. Clancy and the rest of them continue their way to the water.

"The water from the lake is refreshing. I also like the feeling of the humid air on my indigo skin." Looking around, I see that they are of the same mind set. "Alright, we are going tell how you all did." Spin ray says with a hint of a smile.

"First, you all did well. Not only did all of you take care of your prey quickly. It was also done efficiently. Solar and Chloe, you both took out the necks of creatures. While Dawn and Von, the both of you attacked the head. All the methods chosen were ways to kill without resistance." She finishes with clear pride in her voice.

I look at others and see we all are glad to be praised. *"Though that does raise one question."* Looking at Spin ray and Clancy. "Does that mean we can take missions now?" I excitedly ask. Clancy perks up at this.

"Not exactly. You see the hunt was to test if you all can work on your own. However, there has recently have information of a pair drakes moving here. To make sure they don't build a group, you all will take care of them. If you all succeed there will be more missions."

The 6 goliaths are seen moving deeper into the land. There are plenty glowing purple trees. Light blue leaves swaying in the wind. Leaf wings flying in the air. Some of them landing on trees and drinking their sap. Wheel mice trying to escape from flat lizards. Herds of gazelles grazing on shrubs. In the distance there are camels eating different cacti.

"I love traveling the region. No matter what time of day, it's just beautiful." Dawn thought in awe. "Don't you all think this sight is beautiful?" "It is ok, but I care more about the assignment." Von calmy replies.

"Speaking off which, you all will not get any support from us." Spin ray sternly tells them. "This will be your ultimate test to see if you are ready."

"Ok, so it is us four vs the pair of drakes." Solar states. "Yes, however don't get ahead of yourselves. This are full grown drakes. Be careful." She warns seriously.

Continuing their way, they arrive at quartz caves. Walking past crystal bushes, they come to the entrance. Solar starts sniffing the air. "I smell blood." The rest sniff the air. "I guess a skirmish has happened."

Walking into cave they follow the smell of blood. After moving for a while, they find a body of a moth ray. There is claw and teeth marks on the carcass. Hearing noise in the distance, they follow the sound. A small battle is happening between 2 moth rays and the drake pair.

One drake is pale yellow with a thick spike club tail. The other one is grayish purple with a thick spade shaped tail. A moth ray shoots its tongue into the yellow drake. As it tries to drag it towards itself, the drake spits a greenish glob at it. Once it connected the moth ray seized up paralyzed. Lifting its tail up and slamming it onto its head. **Crunch!** The sound of his skull shattering rings in the room.

After dodging a tail strike the other drake spits burning tar onto the remaining moth ray. **Sizzle!** "Argh!" The moth ray hisses as its skin burns under the tar. Light orange skin of the moth ray darkening, as its movability is taken away. Grabbed by its head it is slammed into the ground. **Crunch! Snap!** Skull shattering in the mouth of the drake.

Yellow drags her tail from the corpse. While purple drops the body from his mouth. Looking closely the only wound on the pair is the barb tongue wound. Neither of the pair looks like they are exhausted at all. All around the enormous room are signs of battle. Places on the ground are cracked. Parts of the wall are broken. There is drill like holes in the walls. Large chunks of quartz just thrown everywhere. Craters are in random places of the area.

"This will definitely be a challenge." Von said with conviction. "This will be where we stand back. All actions now will just be you trying to complete this mission." Clancy tells them.

"We already know it is going to be 2 on 1." Dawn states. "The question is which pair, will fight which drake. The yellow drake seems to have a neurotoxin that paralysis targets. And the purple one uses molten tar, that not only burns its opponents. It also restrains them, making them easy prey."

"So, we should pair up appropriately." Solar says with conviction. "With that in mind, I think Dawn and Von should pair up. While Chloe will go with me. You two will fight yellow and we will fight purple."

"I guess that works." Chloe comments. "If we are all ready, let's get started."

The four-started walking towards the drakes. **Crich! Criss! Crick!** The sound of them walking on broken earth rings across the area. The two drakes turn toward them. They both stand on hind legs. "Raaaaa!"

Ness flies down into the small valley. Transforming back into her humanoid form, looks behind her to the remaining dark quill hunters landing. Looking around see notices different plants growing there. Large maple trees cover most of the land. With smaller steel shrubs spread about the area. Fire melon vines are also there in their territory. *"Our main colony's surface area is so beautiful."* Ness thinks in awe. Continuing, she goes into one of the tunnels. Orange plants are all around the large tunnels, metal ores jutting out in random locations. *"I got to tell White spine of what happened with the mission. I hope he will not be mad. I didn't think multiple dragons was going to get involved. I hope I won't be punished!"* Ness thinks in fear.

Walking further down the corridors, Ness passes more chambers. Looking around the gigantic chambers filled with hunters. There is all sorts and types of hunters in each chamber. All of them ready to be sent on the attack.

"I see there is thousands of hunters still here. And many more types than when I was here last time." Ness thought intriguingly. She looks at each chamber, seeing hunters digging more tunnels. *"I wonder what abilities they have. Or how powerful each is."*

Continuing my way, I see the main chamber up ahead. The main chamber is surrounded by other chambers. Around the chamber, there is large diamonds and quilt steel. Walking into the room, I look at all the different types of minerals. *"This place is as glorious as I remember."* I think in bliss.

Looking up, I see the apex on the highest ledge sitting. He seems to be looking at the different alphas he has. *"Well time to report."* I move forward, his eyes catch my movement. Kneeling and facing him. "I have come to report my mission. Oh, Apex White spine, grace me with your ears."

"Oh, Ness I see you have come back from your assignment. You are the only meso to return. Tell me, what is your report?" White spine asks plainly. Looking down at her and nods his head for her to speak. *"I am the only meso here? That's interesting."* "Yes apex."

"I had left with 2,000 hunters, to attack the hikoyasei colony. We entered the tunnels lending to their dwelling. Once we found the bats, we began the attack. While the hikoyasei individually larger and stronger than the hunters, the tunnels helped. They were not built for close combat in enclosed places. So, after killing a few of them, they flew outside. That's where we began to swarm them." Ness informally explains.

"That is good. You use their disadvantages against them. While using all your advantages." White spine praised her. "Go on and continue."

"Thank you for your praise. The battle commenced from there. While three on one the hikoyasei won. However, more than 3 dark quills had them handled. I was on the field, slaughtering all in my path. They were not very challenging to me personally. After killing another one, I was grabbed. Next, I was tossed in an empty area. Apparently, I was taken by 5 larger hikoyasei. 3 of which was twice the size of the average ones. While the last 2 were three times the size." Ness further reports.

"I see, I am guessing they were their chiefs. And I concluding that they were stronger." White spine says with question in his tone. "They were stronger."

"I thought the battle would be easy, but I was proven wrong. I failed to connect any hits on them. They did not have this problem. Their hits connected and I barely had any breathing room. Eventually, I transformed to fight them." White spine interrupts. "I see, they were able to best you in your humanoid form." He evaluates.

"Yes, they did. It was still hard to fight them, even transformed. But I managed to kill two of them. I ate the 2nd one and evolved, fighting the last small one was a struggle. I however overcame it. As I was About kill the two larger ones. I was intercepted by a beam of ice."

"A beam of ice? I didn't know that hikoyasei could use ice." The apex said in surprise. He notices that she shakes her head.

"They can't. While the bat chiefs could use different acids, they used no ice. "What hit you with ice then?" "A dragon." White spine's eyes widen slightly.

"A dragon came and attacked?" "Not a dragon. A group of dragons."

"After being hit, another slammed into me. Once the small struggle was over, I had killed it. The hikoyasei had left, though I think they mobbed and killed a dragon. I had summoned dark quill hunters to distract the dragons so me and some hunters can escape. I am very sorry; I have failed you!" Ness mournfully apologizes at the end.

"There is no reason to apologize." White spine states firmly. "Actually. I am proud of you. Plus, you didn't fail, you completed the mission." Ness looks up with shock.

Ness muttered. "Really?" "Yes, you attacked hikoyasei and killed many. Which allowed you and some dark quills to eat them. Now we have their DNA in colony. All of that was part of the objective. You just didn't bring back any bodies for more DNA."

"His not mad at me? He is proud?" Ness thought in surprise. With tears in her eyes, she thanks him. "Well, it's not like I can blame you for dragons showing up. And them coming during the assault. You would be hard pressed to do anything. If it were two of three maybe it be doable."

"Though, I wonder why did they show up? Does it have something to do with the dragons I fought months ago? Or something else?" "Looks like I will have to take some hunters and an alpha on a mission." White spine mutters with conviction.

"What? Why?! What requires your attention, that can't be handled by me?" Ness shouts shocked and appalled. "Surely you do not need to waste your time to oversee a mission?"

"Actually. I do. This isn't just about making the dark quills stronger. This about making me stronger. Sure, every time you all get stronger, I get stronger. Be as that may, that is only a minuscule amount. If dragons and or other creatures of that power show up, I need to be prepared. So, I need to get stronger by fighting and consuming DNA. And I have a perfect target in mind." The apex say matter of factually. *Especially if they have any abilities and tricks like that magma dragon. What was his name? Blue, Blo, Blood-, ah that's right, it was Blood fang."*

"What are you targeting? If you would please tell me." The question was politely asked by Ness. "Oh, you are interested in knowing?" "Yes, I am very interest." She replied.

"Well, I guess I can tell you. I plan to target golems."

"Golems? But they are not on the level of dragons or hikoyasei." States a confused Ness.

"That is true. They are not on their level. I wouldn't underestimate either though. There is a reason why I am targeting them." Explains by White spine.

Chapter 5

"What is the reason my apex? Is there something gained from fighting them? I just don't see it." Ness confesses. "Yes, there is something to gain from fighting them. You will understand in a moment. There is multiply things to gain from confronting the golems and taking their DNA. One is thicker and armored skin. Another is more biomass control. And finally, weaponize combat."

"Weaponize combat?" "Yes, the golems have an array of weapons." White spine tells Ness. Ness looks at her apex still confused. He nods his head her way to let her know she can continue asking questions.

"Why does it matter about weapons if the strongest creatures don't use any? And how does that make you and our colony stronger?" Ness questions at a loss.

"Dealing with enemies that have weapons will help us. Plus, you are wrong about not using weapons. Remember, if we are to triumph, we will encounter weapons. I need to see were my dark quill hunters stack up. Do you understand?" He asks his tone slightly darkening.

"Yes! I think I understand." Her hastily replies in slight fear. "Also, can I know what you mean that I am wrong about the dragons and other creatures using weapons?" She respectfully asks.

"Well, I guess there is no harm." His tone going back neutral. "Months ago, I fought a magma dragon. It was a tough battle. He had all sorts of abilities. He was able to cover his whole body in magma, making armor and weapon at once. In his hands formed whips and chained maces out of magma. Even a lance and gun shape weapon capable of shooting projectiles. There is no telling what other dragons or creatures are capable of."

"Wow! I did not think a dragon was able to do that. Do you think any of us dark quills will find a way to do something like that?" Ness earnestly asked.

"I plan to fine way of doing that. Once I have, I will try and teach the rest of you how to do it." The apex says with conviction. *"Then, will have more ways to defeat our enemies. Making harder to stand against us."*

Looking around the chambers, deciding he pick from one of them. "Well, time to get some dark quills for the hunt. See you when I get back."

"Wait! How many hunters and alphas are you taking? How long will you be gone? If possible, can I come with you?" She frantically asks looking up at him.

He jumps down from the ledge and lands in front of her. Looking at her he replies to her questions. "I am bringing a thousand hunters and 1 alpha. For how long I will be gone. I say a month max. Also, no you cannot come. Bringing you will just be overkill."

"Ok. Is there anything you would like me to do will you are gone?" Ness digest his answer and asks him.

"No. I currently don't have anything for you to do. You can cover the colony if you want. Or if you find ways to make yourself stronger and bring new dark quills, do that." Turning around White spine starts to walk off.

"What do you want me to do if the other Mesos show up?" She calls to him.

"I want you to tell them exactly what I told you. Anything important they have to say, you all try to handle it until I get back." He calmly instructs her. *"I do wonder when the rest of my meso ones will be back. Seems I will have to wait and see."*

Walking towards one of the chambers on the left side, he goes inside. He announces himself to the hunters. "I need 1,000 hunters to come to me. You all will see where you stack up against others. A thousand dark quills came. The type of hunters that came seem be mix badger and scorpion like creatures. Now that he has gotten his dark quill hunters it is time to get an alpha.

Walking into another chamber with the hunters behind. He looks at his selection of alphas. *"Hmm, which one should I choose? Ah, that one should do."* "Hey! You come here." He points at one of the alphas. The one he pointed at comes over. "You will be coming with me on a mission."

The alpha he chose is made of a combination of a wolf, bear, and troll. It was also bigger than an elephant.

"Now that I got the hunters I wanted and have chosen an alpha, I can go." Thought White spine readily. White spine turns to them, looking them up and down. "Follow me, it is time for our hunt." He marches off. All the chosen dark quills follow him with the alpha in the front. They all pass through the chambers and by other tunnels. Leaving through the entrance, they are now on the surface. Beginning their journey to the golems.

A couple of days has passed. Trudging through the forest and terrain. There are many trees of course. Crystal leaf trees, rot bushes, and neon vines. Walking further in there is a small clearing. In the small clearing, a large lake is in the center. All sorts of creatures are moving about. On one side of the lake a raiju is fighting an owlbear. Many types of behemoths are about. The herbivore ones are currently drinking water.

The behemoths drinking water are bug like iguanas with 3 horns and a crest. The predatory ones are a mixture of groups. Some are bug like reptiles. Others reptilian bird like beasts. The remaining ones are feathered bug like creatures with beaks.

Further away grazing and eating vegetation and fruits are cattle. Not just them but herds of deer, beaked lizards, more behemoths, and grave beetles. Moving further closer to the lake filled with refreshing water.

"This seems like good spot to rest. We can drink some water to get some energy back." White spine looks around at the area. "Listen up! We are going to rest here for now. Go and drink some water to reenergize yourself." The dark quills move forward to drink from the lake.

White spine himself walks towards the lake. Cupping his hands together and putting them into the lake. Scoops up some water and starts drinking it. *"Ah, refreshing. You know, this area is actually- beautiful."* We see leaf fish eating cane fruit. A roll fur trying to escape from a badger porcupine creature.

After two hours of rest, they all get up and start their march. Walking further into dense forests. A lot of shade from the sun. Marching onward for another hour, the apex feels something. *"I detect some creatures nearby. Wonder what they are."*

Two of the dark quills on the right side are snatched up and dragged into the shadows. White spine looks to see what grabbed them. Shadow fur, dark grey skin, and a mole like head. These are shadow beasts. The two that were taking already have their throats taken out.

"Shadow beasts? Hmm, I would kill and eat them, but they seem to be backing off." Which was true. They seeing their others start leaving. "Don't chase them. If they do anymore attacks kill and eat them." He sternly tells them. *"When we walk back this way, I might hunt some of them."*

Hours after that distraction. They all continue to the area that the golems are. *"I think we are close now. Probably a few more miles."*

Looking up, White spine sees buildings and structures in the distance. "Looks like we are here. Everyone, get ready for the assault!"

Richard makes his way out of his home. He is a twelve feet rock golem with sharp teeth and claws. Glowing blue eyes stare at the city block. All the houses and stores around make for a pretty sight. True craftsmanship with metal and stone. Walking further into the district.

"Time to see Tony. Hopefully with good news with the projects." Thinking about why he is out here today. "Good evening, Richard." Says a frost golem. "Good evening to you too." I reply.

As she walks off, I look around at all the people here. There are metal golems, plant ones and other races of golem. It seems it going to be an average peaceful day. Now going by the farm areas. **Crash! Bing! Screech!** Spinning around Richards faces one of the farms.

"What was that sound!? What is happening!?" He rushes into the farm area. The scene he comes across is not that uncommon. A scale cow kicking off an attacker. Scale cows are large scaley bull like creatures. "Oh, seems be fighting of barb claws. Wonder if I should help?" Four-armed bat like creatures with barb tails are trying to attack the scale cow.

Before he can get involved a golem comes swinging a claymore. Managing to hit one but is tackled by another. It starts clawing at his leaf like skin. **Bang! Click!** Not very long it is shot off. Another golem comes out with an elfir gun.

"Looks like I am not needed." **Bang! Click! Bang! Click! Bang! Click!** Killing 2 of the barb claws. The last few escapes by hopping back over the fence and back into the wilderness.

"Looks like more meat." Walking off I continue to my destination.

"I hope there is good news." He thinks out loud. *"Well, I will find out shortly. Here we go."* He arrives at the front door of the smithy.

Opening the front door, Richard enters. There are many weapons on the walls and racks. All types of weapons such as guns and scimitars. There are even grates for bullets. There are all of sorts of smiths working about. *"Now where is Tony? Ah! Is that him over there?"*

Looking over he spots a diamond golem. *"Yeah, that's him."* "Hey Tony!" Richard calls for Tony. The mentioned golem looked up and started standing. "Ah. How are you doing Richard?" He cheerfully asked.

"I am doing alright Tony." He says back to him.

"Let me guess. You are here about the projects?"

"Yes, I am. I was wondering if things are going well with them."

"I actually have good news dealing with the projects."

"That is a relief. I wasn't sure if it was going well."

"Well, it is nice knowing he is invested in our work." Amusedly thought Tony. "I can tell you how each one is exactly going. Do you have the time to listen to details?"

"Yes, I do have time. Please tell me." Richard sits in a chair in the room. Tony begins to tell Richard the details. "Ok, for one we got the resources. We have large quantities of steel, titanium, diamonds, quilt steel, obsidian, and powder. Me and the other blacksmiths have been able to make the scimitars, tridents, and shields using titanium and quilt steel. For armor, we used diamond and steel mixture."

"That is wonderful. Were there any problems making the weapons using this material?" He asks worriedly. "Not at all! They were complete successes. We even enjoyed working with the material." Tony says easing his mind.

"Well, that is one project out of the way." Thank you about telling me about that project." Richard tells him gratefully. "What about the guns?"

"That is going well too. The gunsmiths have made the models of the elfirs as your request." Tony relays to him. The guns themselves are made from titanium and diamond mixture. Bullets have also been made by the gunsmiths." He informs Richard.

"Really? That is nice of them. What material is the bullets made from?" Richard politely asks. *"I didn't think they also make stronger bullets."* He thinks to himself.

"I will gladly tell you. So, since they were increasing firepower, they decided to make bullets with stronger materials. The bullets they made is from steel and quilt steel. Also, you know we got different powder. They did not just mix black powder with gun powder. They also mixed in electro powder, eruption powder, and ignite powder. It really gives a kick in power when put into the bullets and fired." Tony excitedly tells Richard.

"That is very wonderful! I wasn't sure if it could be made with the material. But you all did even more than that. I thank you for that." Richard is overjoyed that the projects are a success so far.

"He seems very happy. That is good. Hehe he." He thought with a laugh. "You ready hear about the final project?" Richard looks at him nods. "Yes, I am ready." "Ok, but things about this one is more complicated." Richard frowns a little.

"Complicated how?"

"Well, making the vehicle itself is fine. We manage to make the obsidian translucent. So, the windows are set and ready. The mechanics was also able to build the trucks themselves." He is informed by Tony.

Looking at Tony in confusion he asks him what the problem is. "Let me explain. So, while the mechanics were able to make stronger vehicles to the current ones. The main thing you ask for is having complications. We don't have the material to make the all-terrain wheels. We did make better wheels. Just not level you wanted." *"Though we are not far off."*

"I see. So, you just need certain materials we don't have."

"Yes. That is right. Once we get the resources needed. We can create the better wheels."

"Ok. What about the fuel source and the turrets?"

"The fuel intake is going well. We were surprisingly able to make the vehicle dual energy." He lets Richard know. "Electronic and solar powered is also manageable. There were really no problems with how it is powered." Tony assures Richard.

"That is great that the energy source is not an issue." Richard thinks in relief. Looking at the blacksmith, he nods for him to continue.

"The turrets are coming along nicely. Even the one for the trucks are functioning properly. The saw turrets are also coming nicely." Politely lets Richard know.

"Oh, that is nice to hear. What sort of mater-!" **Wah! Wah! Wah!** The town's alarm goes off. Richard jumps up and grabs some armor and weapons. "I will see what is happening. You and everyone else stay safe!" He tells Tony commands worriedly. Rushing outside he sees people on the walls. Running up the stairs to get to the top of the wall. Once there he looks to see what caused the commotion. *"What in the hell is that!?"* His glowing eyes widened in fear. In the distance is a mass of black and white.

Chapter 6

After the two drakes let out their thunderous roar. The four goliaths rush forward. Pairs of two are broken off from the four of them. Dawn and Von charge toward the yellow drake. Which leaves Solar and Chloe to intercept the purple one.

Far in the back of the tunnels the two older goliaths wait. Clancy and Spin-ray are far enough away to not be spotted. However, they are close enough to see the battle unfold.

"Do you think they will succeed in this endeavor? Or will they croak and die?" Clancy curiously asks Spin-ray wanting to know her opinion. *"I wonder what she will say. They all have done well up till now."* He hums in recollection.

"Oh? Trying to get my opinion? Why are you worried of what I might think?" Spin ray teasingly ask him. "But if you really want my opinion. I think that they all will succeed in this battle."

"Yes, this battle. It will be their hardest one so far. If they use their minds and plan accordingly, they will prevail, indefinitely." Clancy responds back to her.

"Now, them all remaining unscathed is a different story. These are full grown drakes. A species of S rank level and almost a strong as their relative the dragon. One of our rival species to boot." Spin-ray brings up.

"You are indeed correct. Plus, we know this pair of drakes are strong enough to kill 3 full grown moth rays. I don't think they will leave without an injury." Clancy agrees with her with. Also stating they will likely have an injury.

Me and Von charge at the yellowish pale drake. Both of us prepare to leap onto it. However, neither one of us gets the chance. Yellow swings its club like tail at us both.

Von rolls under the swing. While I jump over the tail. Once I land back onto the ground, I rush forward. Lashing my claws upon his scales and slashing into its flesh. "Arp! Hiss!" Yellow hisses in pain. Backing away with blood cover claws I get ready to attack again.

As the drake seems to get ready to pounce on me. Von hops onto its back leg. He then proceeds to start biting it. "Argh!" With a yelp the drake quickly grabs Von. "Aah!" Afterward it squeezed him and then throws him at a wall.

Dunk! Crash! Thud! "Aah!" Von lets out a yell after hitting a wall and falling to the ground. I quickly jump towards it hoping to do harm. My actions were for naught. I am quickly grabbed from the air and slammed into the ground.

Thud! "Oof! Augh!" I wheezed out in pain. I looked up to see a tail coming towards me. "Ah!" I barely hop out of the way. **Bang! Crack! Crunch!** Looking at where the tail hit, I paled.

There was a huge crater in that spot! *"Oh! I cannot get by that!"* I thought with a small amount of fear. I look at where Von is at. He is slowing getting up.

"Von! Are you ok?" "Yes. I am fine." He wheezed out. "Von. We cannot allow ourselves to be hit by its tail." He looks confused of why I said that. I point to the crater. He looks at where I am pointing at.

His eyes widened and I heard him gulp. "Dually noted." He replies calmly. We both look back at the drake. My eyes open wide. I barely dodge the lunge that came my way.

Jumping further away I go and try to catch my breath. *That was careless of me! I almost got killed right there. I need to focus."* I thought angry at myself. Focusing my attention onto the drake. Von tries to leap onto yellow again but is smacked out of the air.

Rushing forward trying to hit it again. The drake prevents me by swiping at me. I jump far enough from its range. Only to stumble on some rocks. That is all the drake needed.

Yellow opens her mouth and releases a ball of neurotoxins. Dawn is not able to dodge and is hit. "Aah!" She lets out a small scream. Yellow seeing her stunned goes for the attack. However, Von intercepts by jumping onto her face.

Slash! Sloosh! Splash! "Argh!" The drake releases a small scream as Von claws at her face. Being tossed off her head, Von lands. "Dawn! Are you ok?" He shouts in worry.

"Yes. I am ok... It hurt a bit though." She replied sounding a bit tired. *"Thank goodness I am a wood goliath. Otherwise, I would be paralyzed."* She thought to herself. *"Though if any gets passed my armor or into any wounds. I won't be able to move."*

"Hey. Von we need to change our strategy. This is getting us know where." She says as she dodges a slash to her face. Von spits a glob of acid at the drake. Yellow dodges, however. **Sizzle!** The rocky ground is melting under the acid.

"Yeah. You are right about that. We aren't doing much to it." He agrees with her. Yellow leaps toward Von trying to slam its tail onto him. A crater is formed where he once was.

"I have plan. Are you ready to try it?" "Sure, why not. I ready to get some payback." He says with a grin.

Chloe and I rush toward the grayish purple drake. Chloe tries to hit it with a glob of shards. Purple jumps over the deadly glob and reaches out to grab Chloe. I jump over the drake and spit out boiling liquid.

Showing quick reflexes, he twists out of the way. Then he swings his spade like tail toward me. **Swish! Spray!** "Aah! Aah! Argh!" A large cut going from his hip to his shoulder from the sharp tail.

"Ah! This really hurts." Solar thinks painfully. A pool of blood bellow forming from his leaking wound. *"Ah. I must close that wound. Or it is going to get worse."* Covering his palms in boiling liquid presses them on the wound. Sizzle! Steam! "Aah! Ah! That hurt."

After closing his wound, he looks up to see Chloe get snatched. "Aah!" She shouts from purple's teeth stabbing her. So, she returns the favor. "Aah! Ah!" Purple howls in pain. Chloe continues to extend her rock spikes in its mouth.

The drake swings her out of his mouth and into the ground. **Dunk! Thud!** "Oof!" She lets out. While it was distracted, I spit a glob of boiling saliva toward his head. **Splash!** "Aah! Argh!" Purple roars in agony scratching at its face.

I run towards Chloe to see if she is ok. Chloe stands up with multiple lacerations. I look over to make sure the drake is still distracted. Luckily, he was. "Chloe, are you ok?" I ask while looking at her bloody wounds.

"I am fine. This barely did anything." She says bravely. "Let me close them for you. Just know it is going to burn." Solar told her seriously as he walked closer. Moving his palms to each wound closing it. "Argh"

Both turn around to continue fighting the drake. Good thing to the burning stopped affecting the drake. Chloe quickly races toward the drake.

Chloe quickly swipes her claws at him. He shuffles to the side allowing them to move by. This allows her to jump onto his shoulder. There is a reason to plan, ahead of time. Or just to have a following attack.

Anything to prevent your opponent from getting an advantage. Purple is about to find that out the hard way. She proceeds to start clawing through his scales. Digging deep into flesh, bites into and rips a piece of flesh out.

The drake screams in pain and tries to knock her off. Moving all sorts of ways to try and remove her. Even clawing himself to try and reach her. Chloe moves out of the of these attempts.

Moving back to the spot where the wound was. Chloe charges up a huge glob of sharp shards. Once she is finished forming the glob, she spat it into the wound. "Aah! Argh!" The drake screams out in agony. Swiping again he manages to hit her.

Once Chloe falls to the ground. Purple sprays a mass of burning tar at her. Eyes widening, she goes to dodge the burning tar. She manages to partly dodge the tar. She is still hit by a bit of it.

"Aah!" She lets out a scream. "Chloe are you good?" Solar looking at her and seeing the damage that was taken. "Yes." She says back to him. "Your rock like skin helped you." "Yeah, it did. But I wouldn't try to get hit by any more attacks. My armor would not last too long."

"At least you have armor. That would have helped me out." Solar said back with a minor pout. "Quit being a hatchling. You are faster than me." She shot back mildly teasingly.

They both look back at the drake. Purple seems to be finishing closing his wound with the tar. Once that is done, he looks at both with fury. Standing up on his hind legs, he roars. Then starts charging toward them.

"Now that we have made a new plan to fight the drake this should be easier." Von thought with content. He stared at Dawn. And she stared back and nodded. They both rushed forward. Both feigning their attacks.

Thinking that they both were trying to hit it. yellow jumped backed, just like how they wanted. Once her feet left the ground, they hit her with their respected projectiles. Screeching as she is hit and tumbled onto the ground.

The acid burned through many of its scales. While the splinter like thorns got into anything exposed. The thorns digging deeper, the more she moved.

Riled up by being hit by these attacks. Yellow jumped onto the wall. All the walls of this cave are made of diabase. Which yellow's talons dug deeply into. She climbs further up the wall to the ceiling. Then she looked done at them in rage.

"Why did it go up there? What is it planning?" Von thought suspiciously. Trying to figure out what it was trying do. And how this affected their plans.

"Be careful! It is planning something!" Dawn shouted. Not long after she said that the drake acted. Opening its mouth wide open. Yellow started to release an array of toxic attacks. From balls of it to streams containing it.

"We can't allow ourselves to be hit!" Von screamed out. As it all but rained down toxins. Both did their hardest to dodge of the toxins. Any that got close to Von, he countered by spitting globs of acid.

"We can't keep this up!" Were the worried thoughts of Dawn. Throwing balls of wood at the toxic rain aimed at her. She looked at Von seeing him struggle as well. Soon they wouldn't keep up and be paralyzed. Not only that but the toxins are now able to burn through the diabase ground. It would be only a matter of time. They would have to be quick.

"Von! We must find a way to stop this and fast." Dawn franticly told him. "The only way to do that is to knock it down." Von shot back. *"The question is how?"* He thought intently.

Looking around he spotted something. Thanks to all, of the smashing during the fight earlier, there was random pieces of broken rock. Quickly Von turned to look at Dawn.

"Dawn we can use the broken rocks to knock it down." He informs her while using more acid to prevent some of the toxins from getting to him. She looks and indeed sees random rocks. "That sounds like a plan." She states.

They both grab rocks and toss them at her. Yellow stumbles from being hit but stays on. So, they try again but this time covering them with their respective elements. "Aah!" Yellow screeches from the acid and thorny wood. Yellow stilled was attached to the ceiling. The rain of acid stopped, however.

"We have to try something else to knock the drake down." However, it seemed that was not needed. Yellow seemed to have other plans. Which was to jump off the ceiling and swing her tail at them. Both goliaths manage to dodge the slam. The tremor and shockwave were a different matter.

Both being knocked to the ground. Yellow moving as fast as a viper slammed her tail into Dawn. She was sent flying to the air. Before she hit the ground, she covered in wood the shape of a ball. Once she hit the ground, yellow was upon her. Luckily the wooden ball armor held against the slashing.

"Now is the perfect chance to attack." Von after stabilizing himself thought in confidence. While the drake was busy trying to get through the wood ball. Von ran behind it. Next, he shot a couple balls of acid at yellow's back leg.

"Aah!" The drake shrieked as the acid ate through her leg. "I am not letting you get away." He thought to himself as let out another volley of acid. Rushing forward he starts clawing at the injured leg. **Crack! Snap!** Using his claws breaks the leg in half. **Rip! Tear!** Then rips it off.

"Aah! Aah! Aah! Aah!" Roaring in pain as it hits the ground. Its back missing the lower half. Blood flowing from the massive wound. Slowly it tries to limp away. At this current time Dawn comes out of her ball.

"Oh no you don't! You don't get to escape." She said menacingly. Forming extra-long and sharp claws from the wood. Leaping toward the drake she starts to claw at its head. Yellow tries to slash and bite Dawn.

Von quickly, joins in. Covering his claws with acid, goes for the neck. Von manages to cut through its neck. Blood starts gushing out as yellow struggle to breathed. Not long after Dawn impales the drake in the head. Slowly and steadily pushing into the drake's head.

All, of the drake's movement seems to cease. Both Dawn and Von look at the bloodied corpse. Then they look at each other.

"We did it. Yes! We did it." Dawn cheers in glee. Then turns and smiles at Von.

"Yeah. I guess we did." Von returns with a smirk. "I guess we should start to eat the body." "Yeah. Let's. It will make us stronger."

Both start eating, feeding on the corpse with vigor. The taste of drake on their tongues were delicious. They both could feel themselves become stronger.

Purple lunges toward them in fury. Fortunately, they were able to get out of the way. The drake goes and tries to attack Solar. Which continues to escape the assault.

"Ok now that he distracted, I can attack." Chloe thought to herself. Rushing behind the drake goes to hit him with the intent of striking his back. Before she could even strike a tail had slammed into her. Getting up from being smacked away.

"Argh! It sure hurts being hit by that tail." She thought mildly in pain. Looking up, she sees Solar sent flying. Not before he sent a boiling ball toward the drake. Purple quickly shakes the heat ball of destruction off itself.

The then roars at both before standing on its hind legs. Opening its mouth wide open. Next thing that happens steaming hot tar is sprayed out. Straight into the air. What goes up must come down.

"Oh bullocks! We can't dodge this!" Chloe shrieks in terror. *"There is no way out of this."* Thought Solar. *"There is only one thing to do for just a chance."* Solar focused on the literally tar rain.

Chloe extends her rock spikes to form a dome around herself. Solar secretes an oily liquid over his body. Then he heats it up making it boil and steaming.

The burning tar hits the dome of rock. Luckily it seems to protect her from harm. The steaming liquid on Solar is preventing the tar from burning and sticking to him.

Looking over at Chloe, he sees her predicament. *"I see that her dome is holding. However, she is not going to be able to attack."* Solar calmly thinks. *"This is up to me to stop him."* He turns to look at the drake spewing tar in the air.

Walking forward towards the drake. The tar slipping off his body just as quickly as it lands. When the drake was in reach, with no hesitation he leaped on to it. Staggering the drake, which caused it to stop spewing the tar. Following up the assault, Solar slashed his neck.

"Screech!" The drake lit out in pain as he fell to the ground. Hearing the crash and lack of raining. Chloe opens her dome to see the tar rain has stopped. Now she can help and just in time. Solar is slammed into the ground.

Covering her claws in extra rock armor. Same with her hands, she raced for the drake. Balling up her hands she punched Purple in the side of his head. Shaking his head tries to swipe at her. But is burned by Solar who had recovered.

Chloe backs up and digs her claws in the ground. "Hey! Over here!" She taunts the drake. Snapping his head in her direction growls and charges to her. **Crack! Crunch! Slam! Squelch! Drip!** "Aah!" The drake lets a pained noise.

Solar looks at the rock spike that has impaled the drake in the chest. Seeing it continue to struggle. Chloe and Solar both jump above the drake and slam it further on the spike. The struggling finally stops.

Looking back at each other they grin. "That was a fight." Chloe humorously says. "Toughest one I have ever been in." Solar replies in a smug tone. They both turn to look at Dawn and Von finishing their fight.

"I guess we should take a page from their book. Let's savor our victory." Chloe and Solar start to eat their conquest. They all have completed their first step of their journey. What other challenges will they face.

Chapter 7

Richard looks all around the field in front of the wall. All he can see is a mass of white and black heading for them. "What are these things!" A random guard yelled. Looking back at the charging mass then the fellow soldiers. "Start firing onto the enemy! If they start to breach the wall. We must evacuate the citizens." Richard sternly commands.

"Ten of you. Go and prepare the citizens and possibly the livestock for evacuation." Ten golems saluted. "Yes sir!" They moved down the stairs to get the civilians ready. Turning around holding his elfir started firing.

Thousands of rounds colliding with the monsters. Tails, arms, and legs blasted into the air. Many of the beasts kept coming. **Bang! Bang! Bang!** "Why are there so many?!" Screamed a random golem. Emptying a clip quickly reload the gun.

Majority have now reached the wall. Using their sharp claws, they start climbing. "Shoot them off the walls!" Many elfir guns were pointed down and fired.

The firing didn't do too much. Only a small amount was taken out. The first among the dark quills made it over the walls. Tackling a defender off the top of the wall and into the city. More made it to the top.

Seeing the enemy closing in, many guards switched to their melee weapons. Tridents and claymores impale many enemies. This doesn't push them back. The fact there isn't that much room on the walls giving the dark quills the advantage.

A golem takes a swing at a dark quill, only to miss. A stinger through his head is the response he gets. As more time passed more of the guards were killed. All failing to maneuver around and combat the creatures. Richard slices through an enemy and looks around.

"We are not going be able to stop them here. There is no room." He thought in remorsefully. "Quick down back into the city! We can't halt them up here!" Swinging his claymore in an arc cutting a dark quill in half. Richard jumps from the wall onto the city block.

Looking up, the soldiers start landing the ground. Then they started to get into formation. The nasty beasts crawling down the walls. The golems charge toward their enemy. A hunter leaps at Richard, who impales it with his claymore.

Throwing the body off his weapon, he quickly blocks a stinger. Shoving the monster back and slices through another. Spinning around intercepts another dark quill attack.

A golem falls to the ground dead its killer tries to kill another. Only to be shot in the head. The body drops to the ground. A metal golem uses a trident to stab a hunter through the chest. Twirling the weapon she kills another beast.

A sand golem runs forward only to be stabbed in the head by a stinger. Another guard's armor holds out against the clawing of a beast. Which gives him enough time to counter. Impaling it upon her trident.

Other golems are seen killing the monstrosities or being killed by them. "Aah!" A leaf golem shrieks as its throat is ripped out. Whitish blood spiling to the ground.

"Everyone, stand your ground! We can handle this!" Richard informs with belief. Now that the golems are in a more open space it is easier to combat the beasties. Soon they are seen holding them off.

There are bodies all spread randomly in the city square. Corpses of dark quill and golems throughout the place. Blue blood on many spots while whitish blood everywhere else.

"We have done it. We have succeeded in evacuating the civilians." Richard thought in joy, cleaving a dark quill in half. *"We just have to hold out."*

The guards have done their job. With all the people evacuated there is no worry for their safety. The evacuation being handle with vehicles will make much harder to catch up to them.

Then there is the fact that the gate is a great distance from the homes and stores. Plus, the city is huge and would take time to travel. Especially without any vehicles to aid you.

"You like that! Eat steel beast!" Shouting an orange golem with aggression. Cutting down an adversary in her way. "Hurry and die creature." A metal one shoots down a dark quill.

"I think we got this handled." Cheered another soldier twirling a trident and stabbing a monster in the head.

A dark quill leaps into the air to take out a guard. Only for the warrior to twirl in the air and cut it in half.

"We are doing this. Now we are starting to drive them back." Richard thought in earnest. Grinning with razor teeth, he swings his claymore into an approaching beast. *"We will triumph! These abominations fall to our might."*

"Stand tall warriors! Victory is upon us! Let's drive these creatures back!" Proudly exclaims Richard as charges further into the fight. Slashing through enemies left and right.

"We got this! We will prevail! All of us are going to make it!" He pridefully shouts to his follow soldiers. However, his hope would soon shatter.

Back near the gate. A much larger dark quill jumps down from the top of the wall. Towering over every one of the golems here. Looking over to them, it releases a howl. Next it sprints to them to begin a massacre.

"Why! How! What is this beast!" Richard thought brokenly, as many get shred to pieces by the monster. *"No! We must stop it."* Rushing in the creature's direction. "Warriors we must stop this beast!"

White spine finally finishes climbing the wall. Peering over he sees his dark quills fighting. Many of his hunters seem to be struggling to combat to the weapons. *"Hm, my alpha seems to not be having any trouble."* The alpha grabs another golem and bites into his head. *"It seems my hunters' skin is too soft to handle the weapons. Well, there is a reason why we came to attack this golem city."*

Looking over at the corpses, he grabs his dark quill hunters' attention. "Hunters! Feast upon the corpses and become more powerful!"

All the remaining golems look at White spine in confusion. The dark quills do as their master commands them. They start feasting on the corpses of golem and dark quill alike. The guards look on with disgust and anger. "They are eating the fallen bodies!" A purple golem shrieks.

Then their glaring at the monsters ends. Eyes widening in terror as the dark quill skin becomes thicker. Not only that but the skin also has gotten harder.

Finishing their feast and evolution they get back into the battle. The fighting quickly starts to shift into the dark quills' favor. Claymores and tridents start bounce off more than stab or cut. Bullets are doing no better.

"That is much better. Let me join in and give it a try." He thinks pleased that this trip was in fact worth it. Leaping off the gate and lands in the middle of the battle.

Multiple golem warriors stare dead at him. "Let's try and kill him! If we do, it might make these creatures leave!" A purple one screams as she lines up an elfir and starts firing.

A shot manages to nail his shoulder. Looking down at the wound, he digs his claws into it. Pulling out the bullet and examining it. "Hm? Interesting."

White spine then with great speed throws the bullet back at her. Fortunately for her the bullet bounces off her armor. She retaliates with more firing. He quickly weaves through the bullets coming at to her in a matter of seconds.

Lashing out with his claws he removes one of her knees. Falling on her other knee she tries to grab her trident. However, it far too late. White spine swipes his nails across her neck leaving a massive gash. The golem starts to choke on her blood.

Her corpse hits the ground as White spine plainly looks at his nails. "That was a little fun." He muses.

Three more golems rush towards him. "Now this should more interesting." He ducks a swing from one of them. Quickly grabs the offending arm and breaks it. "Aah!" Rushing forward using the arm with sword stabs another with it. Once he fell, quickly throws the one in his hand to the ground.

The last tries to impale him with his spear. Dodging to the right, White spine grabs the trident by the pole. After snapping it in half, grabs the guard and brings him to his knees. Once he is low enough, White spine seizes his head.

The next following second he pulls off his head. With the spine dangling from it. Then he impales the golem he threw to the ground with the spine in her head. Turning around and walking to the golem moaning on the ground. Raising his foot over his head, stomps down.

The head cracks and splashes all over the ground. Before he could think of anything else, a golem rushes him. Jumping to the left White spine avoids it.

"Dang it! He dodged." Richard irately thinks to himself. *"I was hoping to end this quickly. Oh well."* Richard looks down at White spine.

Wondering how such a small creature could be so strong. Richard looks at the creature that barely reach his knees. *"I can't underestimate him because he is small. Clearly, he is dangerous."* He cautiously moves in better position to fight.

"You will fight me." He sternly tells White spine. Looking up at Richard, he replies. "All right then. Let's see what you can do."

Pointing his blade at him, Richard moves first. Swiping to the right the blade misses as White spine backs up. *"Ha! Got you!"* Whipping out his gun fires at him. Not having enough time White spine is shot. The shot makes him stager. Which Richard capitalizes on. His quickly strikes his foe.

Blood leaks from White spine's wound. Blue liquid freely falling from the cut across his chest. The wound closes all the way up after a few seconds. Richard eyes widens in shock.

"Ok. Impressive. Now it my turn to attack." White spine closes the distance in a heartbeat. Lashing at Richard with his claws scratching the armor. Richard tries for the same tactic. However, instead of dodging White spine jumps over him.

He quickly hits a joint in the back of the golem's leg. Richard tumbles to his knees. Just as the dark quill apex goes to decapitate the golem. Richard uses his sword to block the attack.

"You will have to try harder than that to kill me." Richard goes back to attack. Their battle goes on. Both in a stale mate with only getting a few hits on each other.

"You are indeed formidable. I will take it up notch." White spine says with a respect in his tone. Spikes emerge from his arms and wrists. All posing like blades from his limbs.

"Let's see if you can handle this." White spine restarts the fight in earnest. The fight starts to go very different than before.

"How are you doing this!? First you can regenerate. Now you have bone blades that are very strong and sharp. What are you?!" Richard barely blocks another attack.

"Can't you tell? I am an apex." He answers Richard's question. Resuming their battle.

Richard tries to hang in the fight with all his might. That does not matter though. The spike blades cuts through his armor and into flesh. One more clash between his claymore and the spikes leave his weapon shattered.

Pulling out his elfir to fire upon White spine. **Bang! Bang!** Only two shots leave the gun. The gun is quickly snatched out his hands and snapped in two.

The apex dark quill just looks at the golem captain. Looking back at the gun he tosses it. "I admit, that was a good learning experience. But it is time to end this skirmish." Richard looks around and sees barely any of his fellow golems alive.

"Soldiers! Use last conflict!" He shouts sadly. The golems look at him with sadness.

"Yes captain!" They all shout. Tendrils string from their bodies and attach to the corpses of the fallen. The bodies start to be pulled to him.

"I didn't want to have to resort to this." Richard thought sadly. *"Guess I was not giving any choice."* The bodies now by him and line up. Next, they attach to him.

White spine watches as all the golems fuse with Richard. Armor moving out the way so golem flesh can connect. Different armor pieces clacking against each other.

All sorts of types of golem mix, together to make limbs and a body. Soon he becomes a massive being made of hundreds of golems.

Looking over its own body the creature marvels at its form. The creature looks down at them and roars. Looks like the fight is not quite over yet.

Chapter 8

Nine dragons are flying to a clearing. Landing on the cold grass and rocks they all look around. The surrounding area is very humid. Every breath or gasp of their mouths are visible.

"Alright finally. We can check this area and be done with it." A crimson dragon wearily says. Looking at all the large trees that tower over them.

Walking forward a green dragon speaks up. "Slow down. Don't forget we may have to be here longer if there is any sign of the white and black creatures." He quickly reminds him.

Two other dragons groan at this. "Oh. Thanks for the reminder." He sarcastically shoots back. A dragon snickers at the reply.

"Both of you! Don't start bickering! We have no time for this." A yellow dragon interrupts the two and scolds them. "Let's just do what we came here for and leave."

"Do you believe we will find anything here?" Green asks the yellow dragon curiously. "I mean we already checked many locations. There wasn't a single trace of these so-called creatures. How do we know they aren't lying to us?"

"Now why would they lie to us?" Yellow looks at green with disbelief. There would be literally no reason to lie to all the dragons of Mangra Mountain. "There would literally be no gain."

"Are you sure about that?" Crimson joins in the conversion. "I mean they could be up to something."

"Plus, we didn't see any of their bodies. It could all be a lie." Green continues with disdain.

"You both are just tired and upset. The fact you can't realize the stupidity of what you said proves it." Yellow growls back condescendingly, confused why they would be so stupid. *"Seriously, the older dragons wouldn't make up such a story."* He thought to himself.

"Besides multiple of the dragons confirmed the story." Looking back at both, of the arguing dragons.

"They all can be working together in their plot. Which would explain why they were coordinated." Crimson replied earnestly.

"The team was literally surprised when 2 other teams mentioned creatures with similar colors and features." He blankly responds with a deadpanned face.

"Heck. They did not think that it was even connected." Yellow continues. "That is the main reason we are even out here. To confirm more the creatures and to see if they are connected to the beast that has murdered our own."

"I guess you are right. They don't know about this creature or the others." Green finally sees reason.

"Ok, fine. Let's continue with our investigation and see what we can find." Crimson states and starts heading towards the woods.

Following crimson, green goes next with yellow right behind. *"Ah. Finally, we continue our assignment."* Tan thought exhaustedly, she starts to follow the three. The remaining five go after them.

"Do you think we will find anything in this area?" An orange asked the dragons in the back.

"I am really, not sure about that. We checked other areas coming here." Speaks a leaf dragon. "The creatures may have not even come in this direction." He looks at her. "Why? Want to fight one?"

"I would not say that. Just want something interesting to happen." She replies.

They all continue to walk into the woods. All sorts of trees sprinkled about. Along with all manner of plants. Many of the trees here towered over the dragons.

There are hopper behemoths grazing on bushes. Two tusked behemoths are ramming into each other. Battling for rights to use the pond. Baby behemoths nursing from their mothers.

Five tusk behemoths stand on their hind legs. They all are looking out for danger. Little birds pecking and eating bugs off resting behemoths.

In the distance a pack of bug like creatures with barbed claws and large mandibles. They are running after a large frog/beaver creature with fur.

Brown looks to the rest of his compatriots. "Hey. Do you all think these creatures will be a problem?"

"Nah! Plus, they said they took out razorbacks and owlbears. That is not too impressive. I doubt they would be a problem to any dragon." Orange said confidently.

"I wouldn't be so sure. If they are indeed connected to the dragon murderer than they may be on that level. Which means they can harm and kill us." Tan replied.

Crimson turns and stares at Tan. "Yeah, but that is if they are connected. Which they may not. Hence, they are not a problem." Crimson says with complete assurance that these could not hurt anything on their level.

"Let's just drop the topic for now. We all will find out either way. Then all of us can act accordingly." Yellow ends the discussion.

As they go further in, they see blood hyenas chasing a sloth cow. After a few grabbed a leg, it was sent tumbling down. Before it could attempt to get up, a blood hyena lunges for the throat. With ease it tears the neck open. Once the beast is dead the blood hyenas feast on the much larger creature.

"You know seeing the blood hyenas, feed. Reminds me, we haven't eating in a while." Green says out loud suddenly. *"I wonder what is here to eat."*

"What do you all want to eat?" Yellow asks curiously. "Me personally want meat." He looks at the others who all nodded.

"What should we hunt then? What are our options?" Crimson questions them. Looking around they all see different groups of behemoths.

Before they could comment a herd of tree bison stroll in. Large bird creatures with trees on their backs and moss covering them. No wings, However, they have huge hooved feet.

"Well, I am in the mood for tree bison." Tan responds with droll in her mouth. The rest of the pack eagerly nod.

They all fly up and pounce on individual bison. "Erwoo!" They let out. The rest of the herd start running in all directions. Many rushing by the behemoths making them panic. And thus, the behemoths took off running as well.

Landing on the grassy terrain, they get ready to eat. "Glad there was tree bison nearby. They are so delicious." Metal hums in delight. Three of the other dragons agree with him.

"Nah, I prefer to eat click wings. They are juicier." Gem disagrees with them. Then proceeds to take bite out of his food.

"For me, I prefer to eat mushrooms and fruit. I like the texture and sweetness." One of the dragons' states. Looking around the others who are enjoying their meal.

"I don't personal care. Though I admit they taste good when you put them together." Yellow adds his opinion. A few nods in understanding.

"I guess that is a good choice. Different types of nutrients to gain." Tan astonishingly added. Looking around as everyone makes short work of their repast. The remnants are immediately discarded.

Moving onward, they progress further through the woodlands. With a variety of vegetation. Things like blue herbs, red vines and yellow bushes. Let's not disregard the rage apple trees or the starch vines. All around the dragons are miffed. Which is acceptable, they have explored many areas and have found nothing.

They are just distressed that they might be doing this for nothing. Carrying on inside the woods. Grape vines are all over the place. Stretched out over trees or just over the grassy land. Looking up they see animals eating the fruit.

Next to the certain grape vines are spore stocks. And feeding on the spore stocks are fuzz claws. Small roundish creatures with only a pair of legs. They are covered in fur including the tail. Their teeth are flat and strong. Great for grinding and chewing spore stocks for consumption.

Crimson looks appalled at what he is seeing. "What are fuzz claws doing here? I wasn't aware that any inhabited in this location." Looking up and turns to face the others. Some of his associates are just as shocked as him.

Green looks around and examines the surrounding fauna. After his analysis, nods to himself. "It does make sense. With there being spore stocks here which is their main diet. So, any biome in which they grow the fuzz claws won't be far away." He explains to them.

"I am just surprised that they are theses woods. Then again, I wasn't expecting for to be spore stocks." Yellow calmly states. "Well let's continue on our way."

The others all turn to look at him and nod their heads. Passing past the resting creature. Trees cleared out more to show a clearing with rocks all over. Random plants in different parts of the area.

"Do you all think any krakens are here?" Asked Gray as his eyes moves along the environment.

Yellow rotates to look at him and nods his head in thought. "It is possible. At least for the more armored and crab like ones."

"There might be some wyverns here. If we see any, we are engaging right?" Tan questioned in full irritation at the thought of wyverns.

"Yes. If there is any, we will dispose of them. Can't let our weaker cousins get an area this close now, can we?"

"Hey? What is that over there?" Green speaks up and points at something. The direction that he pointed has blood splattered throughout the place. And tiny bone fragments that is barely there.

"Let's go this way. This might lead to whatever created this mess. And if it's one the creatures we kill it." Yellow says out loud to the rest of the group.

They moved further down the path. In close presentiment they all feel an ominous air. Advancing more into the ominous atmosphere. They start to notice something. **Clack. Clack. Click.** The sound of various clicking is heard. The noise starts to get louder and closer. The group of dragons get ready to encounter whatever is going to fight.

Soon a group of small creatures comes around the corner. The mentioned creatures look like fuzz claws. They were even the same size. The only differences being they are fluffy and are white and gray with spikes. The heads of them snap in their direction.

"Oh. Well looks like the creatures are here. The description is a match here." Green looking perplexed comments.

"That just means we can finally do something. Let's go ahead and eradicate them so we can leave." Crimson said in an annoyed tone. The rest of the team nodded.

Multiple beams of different elements crash into the approaching creatures. "What! Aah-!" Even though many died many fuzz quills ran and jump onto a dragon. Within seconds he torn to shreds leaving nothing.

"Keep spraying!" Two more dragons are swarmed and consumed. Nothing was left from them being ripped apart. "Run!" Tan tries to fly away in the air. That doesn't last long as multiple of the fiends launch themselves into the air and latch onto to her. She falls from the sky while being torn apart. Screams not even being heard.

Many of the trees in proximity have the terrors infesting them. Flying near will be a terrible idea. Two of the dragons continue trying to blast the demons away. While the rest start to run.

"Run! We can't stop them!" One of them scream in pure horror. Another one is running in apprehension. The dragons blasting the fuzz quills are expeditiously mutilated.

One of the running reptiles looks back. "Aah!" Whirling around to see the most horrific sight. The savages are almost on them. Soon he trips over one of the rocks in the area. "No!" His screams are silenced as they tear into him. Blood spilling all over the ground. Flesh and bone being grinded up and consumed.

"We just have to make it to the clearing! Then we can fly out of here without worry!" She said anxiously. As they run through the woods, they notice something. Many of the animals have hidden. The ones that have not are seen sprinting for their lives. Looks like they have the right idea.

"Ok! That sounds like a plan." He says with vigor. Looking back as a behemoth is swarmed and eaten. "We found information that was needed. Which will be good to warn the others about."

Light starts to pear through the trees. One by one the trees start to spread out. That in turns makes it easier to move around for the dragons.

"We are almost there!" He shouts in joy. However, dread soon grabs his heart. The fiends have caught up to him. A large amount jumps onto him. "Aah!" Wings and tail are bitten into and ripped apart. This makes him slip into the foundation.

"No!" She screams as more of the creatures get on him to feed. Resuming the escape, she doesn't have much left. She passes through the trees into the clearing.

"Yes!" Is joyfully shrieked by her. Right before she can open her wings, however, she covered by the things. Hear blooded screams don't last long as nothing is left of her. Nothing even remains of the dragon team.

Chapter 9

White spine looks over to the golem amalgamation. Intrigue written all over his face. *"Interesting. I wasn't aware the golems could do this. This will make for a wonderful trait to get."* He gleefully thought before turning his towards his alpha.

The alpha seeing his apex's look understands what's being asked. Wasting no time quickly runs to the golem creation. Within feet of it jumps to kill it.

Right before the dark quill can do harm, its body is grabbed by the golem. Before it can react to the attack, the alpha is slammed to the ground. Following this is the crunch of its body as it crushed. The other arm balls up into a fist and slams down onto the head. With his skull smashed to bits the alpha dark quill dies.

Seeing his alpha die kind of irritated him. It also put things in perspective. *"I need to make stronger alphas and hunters."* He pondered looking at the difference in power. *"My dark quills did ok with the weapons. Nevertheless, the alpha I brought did not even put up much resistance against this combination."*

White spine gives a quick glance over the beast. *"From me glancing at it in this form. I can discern may be equal or almost to creatures like owlbears. Yet not dragons or their rivals."*

Looking at the corpse of the dark quill alpha, he ponders. *"Looking back at Ness's close victory it was thanks to numbers and using advantages that were succeeding. So far none of my alphas can fight something equal to a hikoyasei one on one."*

"Let's see what we can do. Once I kill this thing, I will find ways to improve the dark quills." White spine ends his train of thought and rushes to the fusion.

The golem combination swings its massive fist towards him. He jumps over the grotesque limb and starts running up the arm. Digging his bone blades into the creature. The damage is minimal. Swinging his claws and spikes at the head of the golem gargantuan.

They barely sink into the flesh. Even with the amount of blood pouring it is unfazed.

"It didn't even flinch. I might have to change my tactics." I ponder over what to do. Before I could react, I am punched from its body. Looking up I see a smaller arm return into the collarbone.

"Ok? I am having to worry about that now." Rushing back into the fray. Aiming for the legs, slashes appear on them right before spikes and arms slam into White spine. Quickly ripping one off and slamming it back at it. Just for it to be reabsorbed by the golem.

"This is getting annoying." White spine lets out in his mind.

Looking back at his opponent, he rushes back into battle. Jumping high into air and goes for the being's face. Once landing slashes starts to take place. Within moments he grabbed and slammed into the ground. Handling the impact removes the hand. The fight continues for about an hour. Everything going the same way. White spine would attack and cut of limbs. Only for the creature to pick it up and reattach it. He would get wounds just for them to regenerate.

"Okay. Clearing I am not strong enough in this form." Looking down at his blades. "Time to use one of my stronger forms." Staring right back at the golem.

Claws start to get larger in size. Legs lengthen and extend. The spikes on his back grew longer. White spine's head became more reptilian. The entirety of his body bulked up and increased in size. The form the apex has taken is saurian like. He a third bigger than the alpha was.

Looking down at himself and nods. Moving his eyes back to the amalgamation. In his new form he resumes the fight. Things went completely different this time around.

Claws went straight through armor and flesh with ease. Gripping onto the shoulder blade furthermore with no effort tears the arm off. Quickly tossing it a good distance away. The combination roars in angry but before it could do anything its legs are cut off. The next instance the head and center are crushed inside his jaws. The golem giant twitches a bit prior to dying.

"No problem when I use this form I see." He thinks in his mind. Peering down at his defeated opponent. *"This one was stronger than the rest. I will obtain some nice abilities from this one."* Lower his to start his feasting.

Richard's body along with what was connected to him are eaten. After consuming his meal turns to the surviving dark quills all around. "Eat all of the bodies that are left."

They all get to it. Leaping onto the golem corpses that made up the golem giant's limbs. Razor sharp teeth tearing into flesh and eating it. All the while whitish blood drips from their mouths.

White spine sighs as he looks around. Transforming back into his more humanoid form. Walking to his crushed alpha and examines the body. Putting his hand on it and sighs again. *"The alpha was able to kill multiple golems at once with barely a struggle. However, it couldn't put up a fight against the giant."* White spine ponders.

Flying in the sky is a colony of hikoyasei. The hikoyasei that makes up this colony is the surviving ones that fought against the dark quills. Now they are looking around the area.

The moon shines brightly in the sky, illuminated the surrounding environment. Trees are covered in the glow of the moon. Looking around the coast for a spot. The pitch black hikoyasei spots a large canyon like formation with large tunnels.

"I spot a good area to land. There looks like there might be a cave system here. If things turn out well, we can live here." The black one said. Many of the hikoyasei let out relieved chirps.

"Tsu'tey, do you think this will be a nice place?" He turns to his snow-white companion.

"I think it will Vladimir. The region looks nice and prosperous." She looks back at Vladimir.

The hikoyasei started depositing themselves on different parts on the canyon. Some even touching down on the foot of it. Vladimir and Tsu'tey looks all the survivors that made it. Both peering into a tunnel seeing that it goes on.

"Alright, listen up everyone! We are all going to explore many of the caves. I want you all to break up into groups of twenty. Then check a tunnel and report back to tell us if it suitable to live in." Tsu'tey instructs them.

She and Vladimir go into a cave with a few others following them. Moving forward they see that there are a few different minerals here. There was different fauna here too.

The deeper they walked in the more spacious it became. "Ok, once we are situated, we discuss what has happened." Vladmir spoke up.

"That is a good idea. That way we can all relax and ponder over what happened."

As the group of giant bats went deeper, they used echolocation to see if any hostiles were there. When it was apparent that wasn't any, they moved forward. After about thirty minutes the group heard moving water.

"I hear water. That means a type of stream is here." Vladimir remarks. Moving faster the group lay their eyes upon a large cavern system. *This place is looking more promising by the minute.* Turning their heads to noise that they hear coming closer.

One of the many tunnels which lead to the cavern is where the noise is coming from. They all prepare themselves for conflict. However, they ease their stances when they see what it was making the noise.

A group of hikoyasei strolled in. The group looks up and notices them. "Everything was clear on our way here!" One of them shouts to Tsu'tey's group.

Tsu'tey nods her head at the group. Vladimir speaks up. "Well now we just have to wait on the others." Just after he says that the rest of the groups emerge from different tunnels.

"Guess we don't have to wait." Tsu'tey replies. "Everyone, report to us what you all have seen!"

After some clamoring they all have confirmed the paths are clear with some having some chambers. "Alright. Half of you check the remaining tunnels in the back to confirm if they are safe."

Half of the colony went examine the remaining tunnels. Vladimir and Tsu'tey relaxed and watch over the others. Many started drinking water from the big stream. About an hour later the group returned. A dark gray hikoyasei walked towards them.

"Ah. What is the situation, Felix?" "The other tunnels are clear. With some having chambers or ponds. Nothing that can harm us." Felix explained.

"Alright then let's let everyone know this will be our new home." Tsu'tey turns her head to the colony. "My fellow hikoyasei! This will be our new home! All tunnels here are clear!"

There were many cheers to this news. "Felix, stay with us for our discussion. There is much to plan." Vladimir told him.

"Yes sir." He walks closer to the Tsu'tey and Vladimir. Sitting down waiting for them to start the discussion.

"First, we need to know what happened in the beginning. Noticing how we came near the end the battle. What led up to that point?" Vladimir requested from Felix.

"Well, what had happened was we were attack inside the cave system. I came and saw what all commotion was about." He pauses and looks at them.

"The white and black bear like creatures were attacking us. One on one we can kill them easy. However, we were in fact losing to them." Shaking his head.

"And why were we losing?" Tsu'tey asked. Vladimir nodded wanting to know as well.

"We were too big. The enemy was way smaller and was able to move around. We could not fight properly in the tunnels." Solemnly answers Felix.

"Ah! That is why they rushed to fight in the open." Vladimir nods his head. "That makes sense. None of us, were ever capable of stretching in those small caves. Never mind flying in there."

"Once we got them in the open, is when we started to kill them efficiently. However, it was challenging with them swarming us."

"To make matters worse we couldn't harm the leader in the human like form." Felix says annoyed that they couldn't do anything.

"Ah. Yeah, I remember witnessing many hikoyasei's demise by her hands. That was when Kevin swooped and grabbed her." Vladimir explains.

"Another challenge was what they were able to do. When they ate one of our own, they got bigger and were able to fly. Also, any wounds they had healed."

"That explains our fight with her a little bit." Tsu'tey responds. "After Kevin and Martha was beating the creature up for about thirty minutes she changed."

"It was too weak to fight them in that form. So, it chose a bigger stronger form. Still smaller than us." Vladimir states.

"The organism struggled but manage to kill Kevin. Then she went for Martha and finished her too. After she started to eat her, it's form changed again." Tsu'tey sadly mentioned her underlings' deaths.

"The form was bigger and had similar wings to us. She went straight for James then. After a struggle, she killed him with acid." All Vladimir could do was shake his head sadly.

"Once he had died, she came for us. Only to be halted by a beam of ice."

"Speaking of which chiefs do you think the dragons know what these creatures are?" Felix looks at them questionably.

"It is possible. They came there for those things. The dragons didn't attack any of us but those that killed one of their own." Tsu'tey said in curiosity.

"Those flying reptiles might have beef with these creatures." Vladimir added in realization.

"Anyway. It's probable best not to seek them out. Something big is coming in play. We all should focus on being ready for any future conflict."

"Felix tomorrow you and a few others will explore the surrounding area. Find what resources we have and any rivals that we have." Tsu'tey tells him. After seeing him nod she continues.

"You also are becoming a chief." He looks at her in shock. "Are you sure of this decision?"

"Yes, we are. You are oldest and strongest after us. You are the only one able to do this." Vladimir informs him.

"I won't fail you both." He tells with conviction and determination.

Chapter 10

Back to the savannah, domain of the goliaths. We see our triumph youth filled with glee. The blue light of the moon illuminated the crimson soil making appear purple. The many different lakes in the distance glowed a nice neon. Bushes all over the place with many shades of violet. Hammerheads grazing on mentioned shrubs. Returning home from their journey. They head to the steel like burrow entrance in the ground.

"It's nice to be back. Do you think any of our friends are back yet?" Solar questioned his friends.

"I don't know. I think Calmar's group has still not returned because they went way out for their finally test." Chloe answered

"Emil's group might be back though." Dawn added in thought.

One by one they entered the subterranean passage. Light shined throughout the passages in their underground lair. Many more passages and tunnels were here. Even above them and these lead to chambers. After moving through different twist in turns they arrived at the main subterranean room.

"Hey guys!" A voice shouted to them. Turning their heads, they see a purple goliath walking towards them. Her was reminiscent to a gator.

"Oh, Soo-Yun it's you. Seems like your group is back." Dawn stated to their friend.

"Hi Soo-Yun. Nice to see you are back." Solar joyful says to Soo-Yun happy to see her.

"It is nice to be back the trial was tiring. However, it was worth it." She said back to them with glee.

"It is nice to see her in a good mood." Solar thinks to himself. *"She is just so awe inspiring when she filled with joy."*

"Do you mind telling us what exactly the trial was? We don't mind telling ours."

"Sure, I don't mind telling you all." She informs them. "This should be fun."

"I hope you don't have a problem with me joining in and also telling you all about our test." An orange goliath interjects.

"Leon! How have you been?" Dawn curiously asks him.

"I have been doing well sister. Thanks for asking." Leon happily replies to Dawn.

"Yeah, you don't have to worry about him. He is tough enough not to get hurt." A sand goliath with short tusks says teases. Her skin is a nice cyan color.

The group turns to see that the rest of their friend's group nearby. The one that had spoken was Helga. Besides her is Maria a green goliath with fins on her back. And their elders Emil a toxin goliath with barbs protruding from her body. The grey color sticking out against the brownish orange skin. Then there is her mate Ivan a metal goliath with spikes on his arms. And his skin is a metallic green.

"Oh. There you two are. Do you both mind coming with us to go over your testing?" Spin-ray questioned the two younger elders.

"Huh? Yeah, sure why not?" Emil said lazily. "I don't care." Ivan states laid-back.

The elders all leave to have their own discussion. The group look at their retreating figures. All of them then turn to look at each other and nod.

"Well. I guess we will go first, then you all we tell us of your mission." Helga said.

"I think we all can agree with that." Von said before turning to fellow students. Seeing they all nod, turns back and gestures they start telling story.

"Well, first we had to kill stag horns. Even with their thick hides it was easy." Soo-Yun starts the story.

"Next our test was to see if we were ready to do missions was against clearmores." Leon adds.

"There was a group disrupting the surrounding environment at the mountain lake." Marie says.

"So, of course we had to climb up the side of the mountain to reach them. Which all and all was annoying." Helga throws her two cents in.

"Once we had made it to the top, we saw them. They were murdering all leaf twigs." Leon explained what they first saw.

"The clearmores were also trying to hoard the water. Preventing some from reaching the pond. They were preventing certain lakes and ponds from being able to be maintained." Soo-Yun interjected.

The others looked all surprised hearing what the clearmores were doing. That species doesn't usually hoard water or assault bystanders.

"So as Emil and Ivan stood back to evaluate our performance. We all started the confrontation. After killing a few on the ground, they wised up." Marie continues to inform them.

"The overgrown newts flew up into the air. Then started to attack us from the sky." Helga interjected.

"However, it barely made a difference. Sure, it was harder to hit them because they were dodging in the air. Catching them, our claws still made short work of them."

"That is an interesting assignment task. The clearmores behavior was odd though." Chloe thought to herself.

"So? What was the results of your mission?" Looking at the said mentioned group.

"We passed! Emil and Ivan were proud of our performance!" Soo-Yun exclaimed.

"That is excellent to hear. I guess now is our turn to tell what we did today." Solar said happy for his friends.

"Yes. Let's hear what our mighty friends' task was." Leon said with humor.

"Ok. I will start the tale first." Solar told the others. "So, first we had to hunt sand skippers. This test was to see how we track and kill targets."

"Which they were impressed with." Dawn made them aware.

"After that we were informed that there was a pair of drakes in the area. Spin-ray and Clancy told us that if we killed the drakes, it would show that we can handle harder missions." Chloe added to the story.

Von looked at them and started to speak. "We all went to their den. Seeing a dead moth ray on the trail there. Then we saw them. The drake pair was fighting a pair of moth rays. Which were killed in short order."

"Wow! You all fought a pair of drakes! That sounds like a real challenge." Helga said in shock.

"It was a tough battle. Not only because of their elements, but because of the size difference. However, in the end we won." Dawn replied to Helga.

"How strong were the drakes?" asked Leon.

"I would have to say a little bit stronger than an average drake. There elements were tricky though." Von spoke up to answer Leon question.

"What exactly was their elements? If you don't mind me asking."

"Nah it is no problem. One had tar abilities and the other used neuron toxins."

"Well not we got story time out the way. Let's go hangout and relax." Maria offered to the group.

"I guess you are right. We should relax and have fun." Chloe said back. *"Finally, I can have a piece of mind."*

"I guessing the examination went well?" Spin-ray asked knowingly.

"Of course. They all competently completed the trial." Emil remarked nonchalantly.

"Everything was handled with great flow. Speaking of which, what was your students test and how did they handle it?" Casually mentioned Ivan.

"Our group did an excellent job as well. They executed those strategies of theirs effectively. And I am quite proud of them." Clancy answered him proudly. *"This generation looks like they all will achieve greatness."*

"Oh. That is good to hear. Just proves that this group of goliaths will prosper." Emil neutrally responds.

"What creatures did you both have your group hunt?" Spin-ray asked.

"The two of had them first hunt down some stag horns. After that they handled a group of clearmores causing trouble." Ivan informed the two. "What about you two what did your group go after?"

"They were sent after sand skippers. Once that was over with. We inform of a pair of drakes that needed handling." Clancy calmly told them.

The group were once again on the surface. Basking in the moon's light. An eclipse owl swooped down and grabbed a sand caecilian. It is wiggling all the way trying escape. All for not as one peck to the head ends its life. A sand star crawls all over the ground finally reaching a rock squirrel. Wrapping its tentacles around it tries to pry its shell open. In distance there is light gray lizards with black spikes on their backs fighting gator like amphibians.

"It is just nice to relax and watch the scenery." Maria said blissfully. Looking around at all the animals nearby. Also, the plants in this region.

"You can say that again. Days like this are cherished." Dawn delightedly said in agreement.

"Well, it is not like we got to worry about losing this. I mean which creature could actually-be a challenge and defeat us goliaths." Helga haughtily commented.

"A few creatures can hurt us." Chloe spoke up. The group looking at her. "However, only two are our equals. Plus, anything that could kill us easily is about extinct."

"Oh? What suppose equals do we have?" Helga shot back.

"Our equals are the dragons and the limbpexes. Only they can fully match our might."

"Let's not forget our cousins can indeed kill us in certain situations. Any of the s-rank creatures do stand a chance to hurt us. Maybe not kill us." Von adds.

"Even if we disregard most of the s-rank creatures. We still have the three powers to consider. One being our group which is the amphibian faction. Next the dragons which lead the reptile faction. And finally, the limbpexs who lead the crustacean faction." Leon continues the discussion.

"Granted their cousins are weaker than us. They are equal to our cousins. With moth rays countering the wyverns and colossuses. In addition, tiddaliks counter drakes and karkinos." Solar finishes the discussion.

"Ugh! Fine we are not invincible. That doesn't mean I am going to allow myself to lose to anything!" Helga admits defeat but will not fall against enemies.

"Of course not! None of us would be able to call ourselves goliaths if just allowed ourselves to die. We must fight all of enemies, head on and defeat them!" Soo-Yun declared.

"That is the correct mind set Soo-Yun. We must be prepared." Dawn said to them all.

"Nice to know they can handle drakes. That must have been a challenge for them." Emil said impressed with the young goliaths.

"It was a challenge for them. Especially since they were stronger than normal drakes. Their elements didn't help either." Clancy said back to her.

"Hey! I see you all are here!" A voice shouted. They turned to see a pair of goliaths. One being a metallic type while the one that shouted was a leaf goliath.

"Oh, Calmar. You and Claire have returned. That is great. I suppose you will regal us with your tale of today?" Clancy happily welcomed and asked of the two.

"Yes, we both wouldn't mind." Claire said humoring Clancy.

"Speaking of which how have you all been? Doing well I hope." Spin-ray asked in concern.

"Don't worry Spin-ray. Our group and us have been doing fine." Calmar answered earnestly. "Speaking of which before we tell you four of our groups' examination. We both have a question to ask you all."

"Sure. What is your question?" Emil asked with mild curiosity.

"Do you all know of a white creature with black spikes on its back?" Claire asked them curious of their answer.

"What do you mean?" Ivan asked mild confused.

"I mean just what I said. There were these canine creatures that where white with black spikes on their backs." Claire replied informally back to them.

"You know thinking back on it. We did see bug creatures that were white with dark gray spikes on their backs." Spin-ray said thinking of the small skirmish with the moth rays.

"Actually. We saw light grey creatures with black spikes on their backs." Ivan added pondering if there is a connection. "This could be a new disease that affects different creatures. Changing their pigmentation and making them grow spikes. We must remain alert if that is the case." Clancy warned them.

Chapter 11

The group of seven dragons of finally returned to the mountain. Landing softly onto the obsidian ground, they all look around to see if anything has changed. After confirming nothing out of the ordinary they all go inside one of the entrances. The dragon group is pleased to see no damage whatsoever on the walls.

"Looks like everything is going good here. Let's see if the other search teams have returned." Mist says with relief in her tone.

"That would be for the best. If everyone is back already, we can discuss what they have seen." Scourge acknowledging what Mist had said.

"Of course, those who have survived at least." Calamity chimed in.

"What do you mean? I doubt there will any be causalities. Those creatures are no match for us." Viper arrogantly mentioned.

"Viper, did you forget that we lost Lance and his team? Specifically, to the dark quills." Vein asked incredibly.

"Ok, first one died to the hikoyasei. Nonetheless I do see your point." Viper conceded. *"I completely forgot about that."*

"Even if they don't die to the dark quills, it doesn't mean they are not in danger. Let's not forget there are other creatures that could harm us." Aqua put out an alternative.

"Ok! Ok. I get it. We might be missing people in the end." Viper said frustrated.

The group go back into silence. All of them walking to a bigger room. The main chamber of the mountain where all the meetings are held. On the cave walls bat beetles land to eat the moss. Their four bat like wings replacing the front legs. Soon one of them gets snatched by an ambush worm. After constricting it, proceeds to feed on it. Looking around the massive chamber. They bear witness to its sheer emptiness.

"I guess none of the teams have returned." "What do you think we should do for now Scourge?" Calamity asked her before turning to her.

"Well might as well check to see if the defenders and the hatchlings are ok. Would be terrible if anything happened here." Was her reply.

"Alright then. Let's go see if everything is going well." Calamity and the rest went further into the paths in the mountain. After walking a bit, they arrived at their destination. A green dragon walks towards them.

"Has everything gone ok here? Trouble didn't happen in this place, right?" Calamity sternly asked.

"No sir. Nothing happened to any of this lot here. The hatchlings are doing fine. Furthermore, our territory has not been touched." He informed the troop.

Relief filled the small congregation. *"It's relieving to hear that."* Scourge thought with a sigh. "Can you still show us to the hatchlings? So, we can see how they are doing."

"Yes of course. Majority are in the lower chambers." He stated before leading us to the lower chambers.

"It has been a while since I have gotten to see hatchlings. I miss seeing their adorable faces!" Aqua couldn't wait to see the hatchlings of the mountains.

Several minutes later the squad off dragons arrived. Just for them to witness many hatchlings playing around with each other and adults. The small things being the size of a cow. All their eyes big in comparison to their heads.

Many of them sighed in relief. "Aww!" Aqua let out seeing the little cuties.

"It is nice to behold that our domain with our children is safe. Speaking of which. Has any of the other search parties returned?" Calamity asked the dragon.

"Negative. You all are the first ones back." He explained.

"Alright then. We all should go back to the main chamber and wait for the others."

Eventually, the group made it back to the main chamber. Having heard of feet landing, the sound drew their attention. Looking in that direction reveals Tom's team and two dragons have made it back.

"Hey Tom. I see that you are missing people. Will they be appearing later?" Scourge politely asked.

"No, they are not. They are deceased." He solemnly replied to her.

"Did they die to dark quills?" Vein inquired

"No. While we did encounter some dark quills. They weren't that strong or many of them. It was other beasts that got them." He informed him.

Following his words a few more search parties returned. Some with all their members. Others missing theirs. Few hours later they noticed barely anyone else returned.

"Ok. Since no one has come back yet, we wait until tomorrow to discuss what we all have seen and encountered. That way anyone left will be here tomorrow. Those that don't, we can write off as dead." Calamity stated to those that are here.

Everyone agreed to that decision. There wasn't even a hint of disagreement.

"Following that. We are all tired from our travels. Let's go and rest and refuel. No point being stressed and tired. Every single one of us, needs to be in top shape."

Once hearing that many dragons dispersed from the short gathering. With others going to get some sleep. While others left the mountain for nourishment.

A herd of siderops are seen fleeing for the location. Then out of nowhere many of the bulky moose are snatch up. Vein and Viper both look pleased with their haul. Before eating, they turn to see what the siderops were running from.

Only to see two beasts locked in combat. One being a hybodus, a large land shark creature with dorsal plates and large claws. The opponent is a krypto, a crocodilian creature with rows of spines. Equipped with sharp claws and a thick inner jaw. These two species are rivals.

Lunging forward the hybodus bites the shoulder of the krypto. Before it could press the attack the krypto retaliates. Shooting out its inner jaw into the hybodus. Shrieking it lets go of its rival, but not before swiping at its face. Following the attack, the krypto tackles the hybodus, keeping their stalemate.

"Who do you think is going to win?" Vein calmly asks before biting into a siderop.

"Hmm. I am not too sure. Maybe the krypto." She replies then proceeds to start eating.

The two of them just sit down and start eating their catch of the day. Watching the battle in amusement. Both just enjoying the day.

Deep in rockier spots of the continent, crab shaped stones are seen walking. Right beside it is spider shaped metals moving around. These are calcite and azurite respectfully. Both are living minerals that move and grow. Everything is going peaceful for them.

Calamity slams down and grabs a handful of calcites. Before the rest of the living minerals can run, Aqua crashes upon them. Quickly snatching up many azurites.

"This will be good eating. Don't you think so Calamity?" Aqua questioned her elder. Many of the azurites squirming in her grip. *"I just love the taste of azurites."*

"It will definitely be filling." He calmly answered. "Living minerals are one of my favorite things to eat. What about you, Aqua?"

"They sure are! Many of them just taste so good." She excitedly answered to him.

They both start munching on the minerals. The two of them humming in bliss.

In another location, filled with mangru trees. A wasp eater is consuming hundreds of wasps. Using its beaked like mouth to stab the hive entrance to prevent any of them from escaping. Its long-barbed tongue laps them up inside the hive.

A little further away, a pod of thelyphonid is feeding. The four-armed mammals use their many hands to open biloba. Eating the fruits flesh and juices. Hoots of enjoyment are released in the air.

Nevertheless, those hoots of enjoyment become shrieks of terror. Two of are plucked in front of their pod. The rest of the pod with haste run away. Managing to spook the wasp eater, which too runs away.

Scourge lands onto the forest floor. *"It is always amusing to watch these animals flee in terror."* She thought pleasantly to herself. Looking down at her claws. She kills the squirming creatures. *"Time to get bloody."* She chomps down into her meal.

A chase is taking place in the plains of the area. A group of urvogels are in hot pursuit of something. Urvogels are four-eyed herbivorous mammals with hooved feet and thick antlers. They are currently chasing their prey. Calamites is what is on the menu. They are moving plants that running to different areas for fertile soil and good rays of sunlight.

Some of the calamites have been captured. Many hanging on the antlers of the urvogels and being eaten. In the end though this chase was coming to an end.

Mist perches down in front of them. Following that she changes the humidity making it fog up around the organisms. Once they have stopped and cannot see. She strikes.

With lightning speed snatches up a claw full of calamites and urvogels. This scares the remaining ones which quickly run through the fog to escape. All of them running in different directions.

"Ha! Ha! Ha! That was kind of funny. How they all ran off like that." Mist chuckles to herself.

Examining her catch, quickly kills them. After making sure they are dead starts to eat. Making sure to have a balance meal of meat and plants.

She hums happily to herself. Chewing the food in her mouth, marveling at the flavor.

Hold up in a clearing of ginkgo trees is a group of saurian shape moths. The creatures walking on their hind legs, with no front legs. The wings are replacing the arms and are folded up. Hondricos seem to be feed on the sap from the ginkgo.

Birds are heard in the background noises. The flock seem to be at peace. Only for that to be ruined by a beam of ice hitting two of hondricos.

The ones not hit by the attack are fast on the uptake and fly away. Hydra walks closer to his frosted victims. They try to flap their wings to fly away. All is for naught though; Hydra closes the distance. Casually picking them up in his hand. Once he situates himself, he begins to eat.

A pack of bird saurian behemoths are on the run. The behemoths are being hunted by a pair of owlbears. Then in a flash Roy swipes up a pair of behemoths. This action startles the behemoths and owlbears. Making all parties freeze in their tracks.

"You little behemoths thought you could get away?! Nope! You are my dinner! And you both are going to be delicious." Roy says in glee. Planning to savor his meal.

The owlbears realizing that they are safe quickly capitalize on the situation. With the behemoths distracted they lunge toward a pair. Each one catching a behemoth. The short struggles cease when their throat is bitten into by the owlbears. This snaps the pack out of it, and they continue to run

Roy watches the interactions amusingly all while eating his behemoths. *They were that shocked to see me. Hilarious! Those owlbears sure took advantage of that.*

Swarms of flying insects fly in a frenzy. Hundreds of them buzzing around. A pod of whale like creatures walk forward. The kujira then proceeds to suck in mouthfuls of insects. Each kujira having a feast.

Barely further away giant skinks are chasing down their prey. The scaly elephant creatures try to get away. A large shadow caste overhead. Scaly claws reach down and grabs one of the elephant creatures. Seconds later claws pick up a kujira.

"Thank you for the meal rippers! This edestus will be filling." Jim thanks with snark. Turning his head to speak to Tom. "I see that you caught one of the kujira."

"Yeah. I prefer to eat these. They taste good and they carry a lot of nutrients." Tom calmly informed him. Staring down they see that the kujiras and edestus have fled. The rippers managed to take down an edestus.

The next day the dragons returned to the main chamber for their meeting. Only a few more search teams came back. Dragons look to see all that are here.

"First let's discuss all of what we have seen dealing with the dark quills." Calamity stated for all to hear.

"I guess I will go first." Stated Tom bringing all the attention to himself. "Let me first say that I didn't lose any members to the dark quills".

"Moving on, we did encounter a couple of dark quills. They were quickly dispatched. There wasn't many and they were weak ones. We saw a few small groups before wiping them out."

The rest of the dragons all nod their heads in understanding. Then look at each other to see who is going next. Finally, a blue dragon walks forward.

"Ok. I will go next." The blue dragon tiredly says. "The members that I have lost were to dark quills. They weren't too powerful, but there was many of them. They also were stronger than the smaller ones."

"The reason I say smaller ones is because there were larger ones half our size. With the bigger ones having numbers, it was hard to survive if they mobbed you."

He paused in his tale. Then tiredly sighed before continuing. "We manage to kill them all."

"However, my members were lost in that confrontation. Luckily for us, the dark quills we saw when we were returning was all weaker ones." He sadly finishes his tale.

Another dragon moved forward to report their findings. After hours of reports and findings from many dragons. The time has come for Scourge's team to tell of their findings.

"The dark quills we first encountered were attacking the hikoyasei." Scourge starts with.

"While we didn't encounter any of the large ones. We did find a changer leading them. A dark quill using a human like form was commanding them to attack. It had transformed like the one that killed Blood fang and Scorch."

"We had attacked hoping the exterminate it. However, we failed. It had killed one of our members while another was swarmed. The third was killed by the hikoyasei. The changer and some others had escaped as we killed the rest." She finished.

"It seems that these creatures are attacking everything. One way or another they will attack us. We should be prepared and check our continent to make sure no large congregations are here." Calamity stated seriously.

"Alright. Does everyone agree with this course?" Tom asked the others. Many shouts of agreements were shouted.

"We all have the chance and ability to be ready. We also must make sure the young ones have a future." Calamity said determinedly.

Chapter 12

Twenty golems are seen walking through the woods. All knew they have an important mission. All of them are walking cautiously. With some having a weapon of some kind in their hands. The members of this group haven't run into any trouble in this environment. The only problem being random wildlife.

Speaking of which, there are five of the twenty golems that stand out. One of them being a crystal golem wearing the warrior armor. His weapons are the standard claymore scimitar, trident, and elfir. However, each of his weapons have a blue tint to them.

The second one was a rose golem with the warrior armor. The weapons she used was a little different than normal. She had dual tridents. While her secondary weapons were a pair of magnums.

The third one of this eye-catching squad was a sand golem. Her warrior armor was darker than the rest. She was packing a pair of claymores and an elfir. Which was the same color as her armor.

The interesting fourth was a blue metallic golem. Equipped with the standard warrior type armor. This one seemed to fight from a distance. Armed with a saw elfir and a pair of acid elfirs.

The last, but not least was an oak golem. His warrior armor fit perfectly on to his frame. This one all about close range from the looks of it. Having wrist blades on both arms, a saw trident, the saw scimitar, and a standard elfir.

Those five eye-catching golems were leading the others. All the other golems were wearing the standard guard armor. Armed with the conventional elfirs, claymores, and tridents.

The garrison of golems walked further. Knowing it will take some time to reach their objective. Turning their heads to see a pack of blood hyenas chasing down a tusked behemoth. Managing to surround it, they attack. One of the blood hyenas are gored. The tusk going all the way through its scaley back.

Quickly tossing it of its tusk hitting another blood hyena. Two of the menaces jump onto the behemoth. Fangs digging into the creature's side. Rolling over, the attackers are crushed. Rearing up onto its hind legs, the behemoth roars at the blood hyenas. Feeling intimated the rest of the pack retreats.

"Well, I wasn't sure how that was going to turn out." Said the crystal golem, remarking about the confrontation.

"Hey Jack. Look at this fight over here." The sand golem called for his attention.

Jack turned to see what she was talking about. *"Ah. That is what Liam is talking about."*

A razorback and raiju were battling against each other. Both fighting to their max to bring each other down. "Hmm." A hum came from the metallic golem.

"Who do you think is going to prevail in this conflict, Conor?" He asked the oak golem.

"I feel like the razorback will win. What about you Aiden?" He asks about his opinion.

"My moneys on the raiju. It has superior strength." Aiden says back confidently.

"Strength isn't everything you know." The rose golem finally speaks up. "Who do you think will succeed, Olivia?" Jack asked her.

"I feel like this battle could go either way." She politely responds to Jack.

The razorback lashes out with its claws, cutting into the exposed skin. Letting out a roar of pain the raiju steps back. Allowing the razorback to try and ram it with its tusks. Fortunately for the raiju the tusks bounce off its hardened shell. Not missing its opportunity, quickly stabs the razorback with its wrist claws.

"Rah! Rah!" The razorback screeches as the raiju uses its electricity with its claws to do more damage. Aidan looks to Olivia and speaks. "Looks like this fight is about over." He calmly states.

Not admitting defeat, the razorback attempts to claw at his adversary's eye. It is for naught however, the raiju seeing this, slams the razorback onto the ground. Following up the attack, increases the voltage. Once the razorback is paralyzed it is raised to the raiju's mouth. Clamping down onto the creature's throat. Without hesitation crushes its opponent's throat.

"Well will you look at that. The raiju won after all." Aiden smugly says out loud.

"Don't forget it didn't win because of strength. It won on opportunity and with its electric ability." Olivia politely reminds him.

"Yea, yea. Whatever." He says with annoyance. Looking back at the raiju as it lifts head in the air. "Roar!" All but shouting its victory.

"Let's not lollygag and continue with the mission. I want to be there by night fall." Is sternly said by Jack.

The group keeps pushing forward. Trying to speed up the travel. Glancing ahead they can see the city in the distance. All sighing knowing that their journey is not far away.

"Speaking of which. What exactly is the mission again? I want to make sure I am on the right page." Liam asks a little confused.

"Our objective is to see how the town is faring. We don't know if it is safe or taken over." Jack reminds her. "Captain Richard and the others bought us and the civilians time to escape."

"It would be nice to know if there are any survivors. Plus, if the city is not over run. We could take it back and get the citizens situated." Olivia calmly added.

"Not to mention we could fortify the place better to have secure location." Jack stated. "If not and the situation is dire, we leave further until we find a good location."

"Well, that makes sense. It would be better to retake the city for the people. Rather be in the wilderness." Liam said in understanding. *"Plus, we do have all the animals that we farm with us too. We need them secure as well."*

Moving forward the gang arrive at a more cleared out area. The peaceful quiet is soon interrupted. A barb claw pounces on one of the golems. Claws digging through his armor into flesh. "Ah!" His screams are short lived, as it bites into his throat finishing off.

"Barb claws incoming!" Shouts a random soldier. A pack of barb claws quickly descends upon them. Many battling the golems. One tackles a golem right before being stabbed by a trident. Another barb claw is shot down.

"Hold them back! We need to drive them off!" Shouts Jack. Dodging a swipe from a top arm of a barb claw. He swings his claymore cutting said arm. Then follows up with impaling through the chest. Tossing it off his blade. Quickly blocks an attack of another.

"There is quaint a few of them isn't there?" Olivia questioned before lunging forward with a trident to stab one. Holding it in place with her trident, she impales its head with her second one. She quickly tries to take out another, only for it to jump over the attack.

"These beasts are quint feisty huh?" She says humorously while battling.

"You can say that again. These buggers know how to party!" Liam cheers as she decapitates a barb claw. The bat creature falling to the ground.

"I just want them to bugger off already!" Shouts Aidan being annoyed of their persistence. Using his acid elfirs to shoot at his adversaries. "Squeal!" One hisses in pain as its face and arms melt off. Another one charges toward him. Witnessing the attack, Aidan quickly switches to his saw elfir turning on the saw.

It then proceeds to leap upon him. Only to crash into the saw, its body being cut into two. "How did you like that?!" Aidan concededly says to it. Quickly turning around to cut another in half.

"Why don't you bugger off!" Liam yells at the creatures, annoyed. A barb claw hisses and prepares to jump. Right before it could however, a pair of mandibles snatches it up. Mentioned creature struggles a bit, but it is for naught. Those mandibles crush the barb claw easily.

Speaking of which the barb claw's killer towers over the golems. The beast that murdered the barb claw is 16 ft. Said animal looks like a saurian shape spider. Standing on its thick two legs, while its smaller front arms dangle in the air. The creature's huge abdomen pointed out. And the large head with four eyes, equipped with mandibles and fangs. Looking over at the golems, then lets out a massive shriek. More of the menacing beasts arrive. A sneaky one quickly takes a golem and starts to kill him. Rendering her life void. The beasts' numbers bout equal that of the barb claws.

"Now we are dealing with uropygids? Come on! One pack of creatures was enough!" Aiden all but shouts in fury. Right before firing into a uropygid's eye getting a screech in return.

"We are just going to have to deal with it! Now keep fighting!" Sternly yells Liam. Running between the legs of an uropygid. Cutting through the legs, making it drop and swings her claymore through its head.

The uropygids weren't only fighting the golems. They were battling the barb claws as well. An individual barb claw pounces onto an uropygid and starts clawing at it. Then quickly starts bite and slash away at its abdomen. Wounds stack up and kill the creature, making it fall to the ground. Another fight shows an uropygid grabbing a barb claw with its six arms. Opening the grewsome mouth of theirs clamps down on it.

Jack jumps to the side dodging a glob of silk spit at him. Only to then spin around and slash a barb claw. Then proceeds to do the same at a charging uropygid.

"This is slightly tiring. I wasn't expecting something like this to happen." Conner says exhausted.

"We have too just keep going. We have a task to complete." Jack said sternly.

Cutting their, loses the barb claws leave. That however doesn't stop the uropygids. Deciding to change that the golems start firing on them. After killing a couple more they also leave the area. The golems take their time to catch their breathes.

"Well, we drove them off. Now we can continue as planned." Olivia says optimistically.

"Yeah. You are right, shall we continue?" Jack whole heartly agrees with her.

"Yeah. Let's do that." She replied in kind. As everyone gets ready to leave Conner speaks up.

"What are we going to do about the bodies?" Jack turns to him and thinks to himself before looking at the two bodies.

"Nothing much. One is unsalvageable while the other is. However, we do not have the luxury to give a burial. Now if we can take back the town and his body is still here, we can." Jack explained.

"Speaking of which. Once we are a few miles away we will rest. That way the injured can attend to their wounds. This will also give time to eat and drink." He informs the group.

"Understandable. We can't push ourselves too far." Olivia states in agreement. *"I am actually surprised we only lost two warriors."* Proud of the outcome, she hopes this continues.

Trudging in the foliage to reach the city. Everyone knows that one way or the other this mission well help them. Whether or not they get the most desirable outcome is left to be seen.

Following them traveling a few miles, all glance and see that there is not much left to go. Slowing down the troop check to discern if it is safe here. Proceeding to repose the gang start to get comfortable.

"Ok, this is an acceptable spot to get some respite. Everyone, treat your wounds and consume any nourishment that you need." Jack calmy orders peering at his troop.

Numerous of the golems started to apply first aid upon their injuries. Some even hissing in pain from applying the medicine. Multiple containers of food are opened. In addition, metal bottles are unfurled to quench their thirst.

Aidan bites into his dried meat and consumes it. "Just what I needed." He uttered in bliss.

"Yeah. Filling an empty stomach is great." Liam vocalized in consensus. Proceeding to eat an apple.

"I believe handling one's thirst is more relieving." Announced Conner as he downed some of his water.

"Both are equally refreshing. There are certain pleasures you get from both." Olivia remarks in compromise. Munching on her carrot then drinks some of her water.

Gnawing on his jerky Jack turns to glance at the others. While multiple of the soldiers were eating their food or drinking from their canteens. He couldn't help but look in the distance where the city is located. Sighing at the journey ahead.

"At the end of the day. What really matters is staying alive." He comments in seriousness.

"Well, you are not wrong. Keeping your life is what is most important." Olivia full heartly confirms.

Everyone starts to finish up and prepares leave the location. Repacking their supplies, they move onward. Traveling through so many plants that were in the way. Presently after traveling a few miles, they arrive at one of the city's walls. Staring up, the group knows what they must do.

"Are you all ready? To see what the situation is. There is no telling what will happen in these walls." Jack asked his troops. All the warriors the shout their encouragement.

Chapter 13

In a grand field there are many organisms basking in the sun. Others are on their own in the area. Iguanodons are drinking from the massive lake. While trice behemoths are battling with each other using their huge 3 horns to ram each other. Further out there are meadow leopards feeding on some of the corn crops. In addition, with plenty of walking logs laying all about in the sun.

This is the scene that greeted Felix and his group of hikoyasei. Many of the group were at awe at the scene. *Well, this place is already looking promising.* Felix thought in his head.

"Wow! This place is wonderful. Our new home is great." A purplish one exclaimed in cheer.

"I wouldn't be celebrating yet. We still don't know what threats are here." An orange hikoyasei with stripes stated.

"Clive is correct. We are out here specifically to check out any threats." Felix vocalized. "In addition, we are to see what resources this region has to offer."

"Will we be bringing back any food?" Clive asked.

"Yes. After scouting part of the area, we will break back some food for colony. We also will be able to feed on such food." Felix remarked.

"Ok sir. I guess we seen what we needed to here."

"That is correct time to check the other locations." Declared Felix no longer staying in place.

The group flies further over the meadows. Reaching the areas with trees. Small mammals are all frolicking on the branches. Now in the more forest spot do they examine more of their surroundings.

Looking around at all the different kinds of trees around. A large river cuts through the territory. With animals on both sides of the river. On one side there are iguanodon resting by the river's edge. Just absorbing the sun's rays.

"This looks like another great hunting spot." Felix muttered eyeing the river for threats.

Staring down he sees all manner of fish swimming. Large ones that could be a decent meal. A shadowed shape swims to the edge of the river where the iguanodon is at.

"What is that?" Clive asked curious.

Once the shadow reaches the edge, it bursts from the water. The iguanodon jumps back. As a huge leech with legs stares at it. "That Clive is a koolasuchus. Nasty little things." Felix informs him.

Just then another koolasuchus leaps out of the water. The iguanodon runs for its life. With the koolasuchus hot on its tail. Fate would have it that the iguanodon's life should come to an end. One of the koolasuchus manages to latch on. Dragging its prey to the ground. In no time another head latches on. Life leaving its body, its nothing more than a meal for the leeches.

"You are right! They are vicious. Draining its blood and ripping it apart." He voiced in shock.

All of them started flying off, as the pair of koolasuchus wildly tear their prey apart. Glancing over at the other side of the river. There lots of trees, many being dark apple trees. Large blue and black apples blooming on their trees.

"Ooh! Dark apples! Yes, they are going to be delicious!" One of the hikoyasei squealed.

"Hold your acid now. We ought to check this territory to make sure everything is fine." Another gruffly mentions.

"Yea. Yea. But if everything checks out, then the apples are the first thing I am snatching up."

"Fine, whatever." He relented.

Soon the trees start to spread out, allowing them to see the forest floor. Movement is spotted, which grabs their attention. Down there on the forest floor a bipedal fish was eating sugar melons from the vines. Full on invested in gaining their nutrients. A good chunk of this area seems to be full of sugar melons. This unknown landscape seems to have an abundance of vegetation. With large amounts of fungi and small creatures. Animals such goats, buffalos, and hedge crickets.

"Wow, just look at this place. This bio is just perfect and there are grass skippers here. That is good eating right there." Said one of the hikoyasei spoke in awe.

"You do have a point. I think the chiefs will be pleased with this information. Luckily, we have yet to find a serious threat to us and the colony." Felix in agreement spoke. *"All we have to do is confirm there are no threats."*

"All right, listen up! We only have three more locations to check for today. Succeeding the mission, you all will bring back some food for the colony and yourselves. Remember the extra is food is going in storage for later." He announced. "Some of it will be eaten today but we are going to start our routines again. Once everything is rolling well everyone will hunt or guard the children."

"Yes sir!" Clive and others responded.

"I hope I get to eat more of what I catch. I don't like sharing." A voice whispered.

"Oh, calm down. It is only temporally." Another chided the voice.

Resuming their flight, they're flying into the next bio. Peering at all the scattered trees, Felix pondered to himself. *"Since they can joke around, that means they weren't too shaken about what happened. Good. They need their heads in the game and to prepare for anything."*

"Pa-woo!" Everyone's head snaps downward to the noise. Elephants are seen running through the trees in clear distress. All but screaming in pure terror. Any small trees in the way are crushed and snapped out of the way.

"What got those things so worked up?" Clive questioned out loud.

However, his answer came quick. A flock of avian animals are chasing them. Different from normal birds these creatures have massive forelimbs. Equipped with razor sharp talons. While not having any wings or legs. Baring a serpent like tail with quills on the tip. Quills also on the back, arms, and with a quill crest.

"What type of birds are these?! They are not normal looking!" Clive exclaimed in shock.

"Those are rocs, Clive." Felix answered while observing the flightless birds. "They are a species of predatory birds. With no remorse for their prey."

"Are they a threat to us?" One of the others questioned.

"One on one, no. Only the real old ones can handle us solely." Felix informed them. Unfortunately, he wasn't done. "Their numbers are what is dangerous. While they prefer to hunt solo, they will gang up on anything larger than them. They are also a little intelligent, knowing how set traps." He finished.

"So, these are one of the creatures to warn the chiefs about?" One of them asked.

"They are of note. Though we probably don't have worry about them attacking our foundation. Unfortunately, hunting near them might be a problem." Felix explained to them.

One of the rocs lifts its tail and flings quills at an elephant. Squealing it topples over from the barbs in its back. Reaching its victim, starts tearing into it. Another roc runs faster and leaps onto an elephant. Talons stabbing right through its skin, holds it in place. With precision peaks into the elephant's skull.

"As you can see, they are ferocious animals. Stopping at nothing to get their prey. Unrelenting." Felix comments.

With the teeth shapes hooks in their beaks, the rocs rip out flesh and consume. More of the elephants are caught and killed. Blood all over the faces of these killers.

Clive turns to Felix to say something. "Can we walk for the rest of the expedition. That way we can rest our wings." He requested.

Felix staring at him responds. "Sure. We are flying our way back. And we have been flying the hold time."

After multiple cheers they land. Checking the trees all around, start to walk. All around there is a peaceful atmosphere. Trees having grown huge thanks to all, of the sun's rays. Of course, not to forget the fertile soil all here. Which is what lead to all manner of plants growing here. Including the moving plants here.

Many of said plants are walking around before settling into the soil. Moving fungi crawl all over the fallen trees and logs. Small creatures munching on the grass and leaves.

Regretfully the peaceful nature ends. All thanks to the sprinting herd of rhinos. The group of hikoyasei all but stare at the frightened rhinos. All but wondering, what could have spooked them. It didn't take long to get their answer.

A troop of large mammalian predators are chasing them. Most of them running upright on their legs. While others are on all fours using their knuckles. Thick patches of fur on the back of the neck through the spine all the way to their club tails.

The rest of the body was furless. Thick muscular skin was in place of the fur. Razor sharp claws adore the hands of the creatures. Upon said beast head was a head crest of horns.

"Oh. I was not thinking there would be berserkers here." Felix said in surprise. Eyes blinking in shock.

"I heard of berserkers, are they that dangerous?" Clive piqued in with a curious expression.

"Well, yes and no. My shock is more of the fact that they live here vs their threat level. Make no mistake though they are very capable." Responded Felix to Clive's inquire. "They are physical stronger than animals above their weight class. Such as owlbears, raijus, and razorbacks. In comparison though, they are not as durable or intelligent."

Felix examines his group, ensuring that they were following along. After confirming this was in fact the case, he continued. "Meaning in an outright fight, it depends on who gets the most hits to decide the victory. That's not including the fact that they do not have a special ability like the mentioned creatures."

"What do you mean about that?" A purple hikoyasei asked confusion in her voice.

"What do I mean about it? What I am talking about is that berserkers don't have electricity or lightning like raijus. They are not elemental beasts like owlbears. Or have spiked quills for defense and offense attacks like the razorbacks." He finished clarifying for her.

"Their only weapons are their claws, clubbed tail, horns, and teeth. Now they are in fact capable of using the environment around them. However, that is hardly helps them against things above its class unless it is a strong material." He further informs them.

Berserkers are creatures based more on instinct than anything else. That is not to say that they are dumb. They are just hands on animals. While they are capable of breaking and destroying things that certain more powerful creatures cannot. Or in fact deal more damage to adversaries.

Their lack of intelligence means they can be lead around. Plus, their defense does not hold out to creatures like the razorback. Then again, the fact it can hit above its weight class is remarkable enough. When it comes to fighting anything on its level or lower, they normally win.

"Now they not outright dangerous to us. Those claws can hurt us though so try not to get hit by them. It is also not hard to trick them." Felix told in consideration.

Going back to regarding the berserkers. They have seemed to have cut off the rhinos' escape. Surrounding the herd, they move closer. Many of the herd attempt to fight back. That plan is foiled without delay. Each one of the berserkers swing their arms at their prey.

Claws ripping straight through flesh with no resistance. Blood flying all in the air. Squeals of the dying rhinos reverberate in the forest. With the last pained moan of the dying, no breath comes from the herd. Wasting no time, the berserkers dig in. Feasting on their kill.

"That was brutal and bloody." Clive states a little ill from seeing the barbaric murder.

"You could say that. At the end of the day though it was efficient. They could not run away, and they were killed quickly." Clive was reminded by Felix. Not wanting to be reprimanded he nodded his head.

"Now everyone! We are going to rest a bit. I will allow you all to go and find yourselves something to eat. Once we all are done resting, we will continue to check one more place, then we are returning. Is that clear?" Felix announced to them all.

After hearing multiple yeses, he dismissed them all. Felix walked through a part of the forest and found a stream. Moving closer to the stream decides to get a drink. Lowering his head, he starts to lap up water.

"This is refreshing. Been a little bit since I had water." Felix couldn't help but think.

A little later, after having his fill starts to look for food. He watches as one hikoyasei tackles a grass skipper. Proceeding to claw into it and then feasting. Another one captures a type of behemoth. All while a few lay on their backs eating different types of fruit.

Shaking his head at them he continues to search for food. Quickly snatching up a siderops. Finding some fruit takes that as will. First biting into the siderop. He hums as the blood fills his mouth. Chewing on the flesh with a pleased look.

Once halfway done turns to bite the fruit. Mewling in bliss at the sweet taste in his mouth. Happily chewing on his fruit. His mind goes over what has happened today. Wondering what else will come.

Chapter 14

Eight goliaths make their way back in the underground systems. The sound of their chatter bounces off all around the walls. Enjoying their time together, the group off friends go to relax in one of the chambers.

"Well, I have to say that all of our adventures were interesting." Leon causally stated.

"Now, what is this I hear about interesting adventures?" An unknown voice asked.

Everyone turns around to see the speaker. The speaker is a black goliath with purple spines. "I would love to hear about them!"

"Disregard Oliver. He just hyped about the mission we completed." A white colored goliath with orange fins on her back. "You know how he gets." She dismissively.

"Come on, Ilya! You don't have do me like that. I just heard them talking about assignments and wanted to know." Oliver retorts looking at Ilya for the comment. "River, Lily back me up here."

The mentioned goliaths are both looking like they don't want anything to do with this. One is a spikey goliath, and the other is a peach goliath. Both were named River and Lily respectfully.

"While I do understand where you are coming from. That was a little extra." River replied stoically.

"I just want nothing to do with this." Lily calmly stated.

Oliver puts his hand on his chest in mock hurt. "You both wound me. The betrayal." He said with a laugh.

"That is alright. Plus, I find it amusing when he acts all boisterous." Solar told them; happy his other friends are here. "Anyway, I see all you are back now."

"Yeah. Our evaluation was a little challenging. In the end though we handled it." Oliver said with a grin.

"Oh, really? I bet you all struggled. Barely passing too." Helga snorted and laughed at them.

"Funny. That sounds like you when you are doing anything." Ilya shot right back at her.

"You are one to talk bitch. You do nothing right!" Helga said pissed off. All but staring daggers at Ilya. Right before they could escalate the situation, Solar intervened.

"Now the both of you calm down. There is no reason to fight." Solar stated calmly. *"Man, these two are a handful when they are together."* He thought tiredly.

"Yeah! Let's stop with y'all barking so we can hear what their teams did." Said Oliver. Looking at his fellow goliaths expectantly.

Solar raised his brow at the gaze then chuckled. Leon then walked up and asked. "You want to know about our mission?" *"I didn't think he would be interested."*

"Of course. Plus, after you all tell us about your test, we will tell you about ours. You 3 are fine with that right?" He says turning to his team. Lily nods while River shrugs. "I am fine with it just don't expect me to be the main one talking." Ilya told him.

"Ok. I am fine with being the main speaker. So Solar, Leon what do you all have to say to my proposal?" He looks to them both and their groups.

"I am personally ok with it but what about you all?" Solar states before asking his teammates. Glancing at them all he only receives nods from them. Nodding back to them, turns back to Oliver. "Well, you got our answer."

Both Oliver and Solar shift to view Leon. Who seems, to be pondering about the suggestion. Nodding to himself looks to them. "I don't see a problem with it." Glancing back to his group. Soo-Yun and Marie just nod. "I can get behind this. This will show them how much better we are them!" Helga adds her answer.

Ilya snorts at her. Leon smiles at his team. "Ok, we are in as well. Now it is up to us figure out who goes first." Leon turns to Solar.

"I am fine with you all going first." Solar tells him. Leon nods his head then looks to Oliver's team.

"With that out the way, Let's tell what we been up to." After about thirty or so minutes of speakers switching and talking their tale was told.

"While the stag horns weren't that interesting or challenging the sound of the hunt sounded fun." Oliver spoke up. "Now those overgrown flying caecilians sounded more of a problem."

"Yeah. Besides the annoying numbers they had. They mainly tried to attack from the air." Soo-Yun said a little irked.

"Ok. Nice objective and congratulations on passing." Ilya praised them. Then she and her crew turned to Chloe's group. "Ok, your turn."

"Alrighty then. So, this is what we did." Solar starts to recap what they had to hunt and fight. Forty minutes of explaining what they went through, they were done. Oliver and his team looked at each other then nodded. All of them clapped for Solar's team's trials. They smirked at the clapping.

"Ok, I must admit that was that was a fully equipped set of trials." Ilya stated.

"Your whole evaluation was almost as interesting and challenging as our hunt and objective." Oliver said a little bit cocky. All of them turned to him with varying expressions.

"Oh yeah! What did you all do then?" Helga said heat fully. Snarling a little at them.

"I will gladly tell you all." Oliver starts to inform them of what happened.

Trudging through a thick marsh was a squad of goliaths. Lily looks all around with a joyous expression. Calmar looks at the younger goliaths with pride in his heart. They really have come a long way.

"Oh, marsh water just feels great on the skin. I love going to marshes." Lily hummed out.

"If you say so." Oliver responded. *"She really likes marshes."* He thought to himself.

"Do you not like the waters of a marsh? Or marshes in general?" She asked in return.

"I don't care one way or the other for either." Was his response. Lily turns to Ilya and River. "What about you two?" "Not the worst place, I have been." "I really don't care." Were their responses.

"Ah. I wish that you all would have liked this as much as me." She whined.

"Don't get to cozy! You all are on a mission here. Do you remember your mission?" Claire sternly reminds and questions.

"Yes ma'am! We are to kill or repel a large pod of kryptos that have moved into the area." Oliver answered her. "There are too many of them in this area which will mess up the marsh ecosystem."

"Good you are aware of y'all's assignment." She says pleased with his answer.

"Don't forget that you four will be doing this by yourselves. We will not help, even if you are about to die." Calmar adds in.

"Yes sir!" They all shout and affirming that they are aware of this fact. Once they moved closing into the marsh forest Calmar and Claire stop moving. "This is as far as we go. We will be watching from a far so try not doing anything embarrassing." Claire informed them.

They all gaze at each other and nod. After looking at the older goliaths they resume walking. Trudging through the wet grass and small plants they hear a noise. Upon closer examination they confirm the noise is their targets. There in the distance is a huge number of kryptos.

"Finally. It's show time." Thought Oliver eager to complete their task. "Alright, are you all ready. This party is about to turn up." He questions them.

"You bet! We are about to make this a blood bath." Ilya cheered with the other two showing their support.

"Let's prevent them from ruining the marsh!" Lily exclaimed.

With the affirmations the group of goliaths prepare for conflict. Speeding up they descend upon them. River quickly grabs one by the head. With no effort tears the head off. Seeing the commotion, the rest of the pod attacks.

However, the goliaths are ready. Fighting back and killing kryptos left and right. Claws and fangs biting and tearing. Lily bites one on its neck before crushing it.

River impales one through its shoulder then with quick speed throws it at another. Two kryptos jump on Lily. They are quickly tossed off. Oliver snatches one up and rips its jaws apart. A bunch pile on top of River.

"River!" Shrieks Lily in terror. Oliver just looks back.

"He is fine." He says nonchalantly. As if proving his point spikes impale the crocodile creatures.

River shakes the died bodies off him. "See, what did I tell you"

"Ah! These things are annoying!" Ilya yells as a pair of kryptos skewer her arms with their inner jaws.

Oliver soon joins her in annoyance as a krypto shots out its inner mouth and punctures a leg. Ilya starts having a type of slime secrete from her. Once it touches her assailants it explodes. Blasting them to bits. While Oliver just steps on his attacker crushing it underfoot.

Oliver turns to River catching his eye. "River spike rain!" He nods and runs toward him. He jumps onto Oliver's hands and is tossed into the air. Barely a moment later hundreds of spikes are hurled from his body and impales their enemies.

Now with some breathing room Ilya covers some lumps of plants with slime. Then tosses them at the krypto pod, blowing them up. Following this action Oliver shoots projectiles from his mouth. Sniping the crocodiles left and right.

There is silence in the marsh. Nothing or anyone making a sound the kryptos and the goliaths stare at each other. After moments of a tense stare down the kryptos flee from the marsh.

The group stare at the retreating kryptos. Eye bawling them as they left. Once they have completely vacated the premises. They all turn and peer at each other. A moment later than sigh.

"Looks like that is over." River says.

"You are correct in your assessment." A familiar voice called

Turning around they are greeted with the sight of Calmar walking towards them. With Claire behind him. He stares all around them and nods.

"Great work. You killed a good amount of them. While driving off the rest. Now any that live here will be an appropriate number." He claps proud of their achievement.

"Don't relax yet. You have another task to complete." Claire informs them. The four looks at her.

"What is our next task?" Oliver asked

"You all will exterminate a wyvern nest." She clarifies. Turning to face them probably. "There are too many growing and are too close to our home."

"If there were less numbers or they were further away we wouldn't care." Calmar added. "However, that's not the case."

"Ok. So, we are going to head to the nest. Then every single one we kill?" Oliver questioned.

"Affirmative. Though if any do flee the region you don't have to worry about them." Calmar explained.

"With that everything is cleared up." Claire started talking. "You all are allowed to go ahead and eat your kills. That way you have more energy to fight."

"Yes ma'am!" Shouted the younger members of the group. Each proceeded to reach for a krypto. Lifting their quarry, they each bite into their food. Once it has been ten minutes, they finish up eating. Turning to the older goliaths they nod.

Now that everyone is situated, they prepare to locate the wyverns. They all march out of the marsh. Moving through more forest surroundings they around for markings.

"Don't worry. Once we get to more-rockier terrain we will be close. That is the location where the nest is." Calmar told them.

"Well, I guess that is one less worry for our minds." Oliver thought in his mind.

"Actually; this is good news; I prefer rock terrains. I don't like fighting in forests." Ilya happy with this development.

River seems to be thinking about something. *"I will have to be careful with my spikes. Don't want them to stab me or my friends. Then again, I could also use this to my advantage."*

"Well, it will be easier to use my abilities there than in the forest." Lily pondered but still a little upset it couldn't be in the marsh.

Walking further into the forest, the grassy floor started becoming rocky. After a while there mainly stone everywhere. Looking further in they spotted the nest. There were two full grown wyverns. They were not alone either. There were many smaller wyverns crowded around them.

"This will be where Calmar and I will be stopping. Remember to be cautious and to not show off. Use all of what you need to use to win. Oh, and do try to come back alive. Good luck." Claire coldly told them. "Yes ma'am." They all replied. Turning to face the wyverns.

Chapter 15

The group of golems walk up to the wall. Jack peers up to the top calculating the time it will take to get up there. Many of the golems' gulp or sigh at the idea of climbing.

"Alright everyone give heed! As you all are aware, we are going to have to climb the wall to access the city." Jack looks over to everyone gathered. "Once we get over, we will begin our investigation. If all goes well, we will inform the others and unlock the gate for them to enter. Is everyone ready?"

Everyone nods their head. Opening the equipment so they can start the climb. Olivia walks up to Jack. "How long do you this will take?" She politely questions.

"Minimum 30 minutes. If this drags out, then an hour. Either way we will be in the city way before nightfall." He informs her after consideration.

"That's great! I don't want to have to take all day." Aidan deadpanned. Shaking his head, he shoots the top with a hook. Tugging the rope to make sure it is secure.

"Oh, quit your bitching. And start climbing. The sooner the better." Liam snapped annoyed at his antics. *"Always whining about something."*

"Oh, shut your fangs. I am climbing." Everyone had their grapplers secured. Climbing the rope up the wall their climb begins. Jack, Olivia, Liam, Aidan, and Conor were climbing with ease. The other golems were struggling a bit with the climb.

"I am going to enjoy the view from the top when we make it there." Aidan stated looking down.

"I guess that would be interesting. However, focus on the mission." Jack said moving further up the wall.

"So, how do you think it is going to go once we make it inside the city?" Liam asked. Looking at her companions with her feet pressed onto the wall.

"Well, we are going to split up into pairs. With how large the city is we going need cover more ground." Olivia politely told her. "We have to make sure there are no threats in the city." She adds.

"And of course, we are going to walk. Which will take time." Aidan bitterly said. "Wait if we find any working vehicles can we use them?" He asked hopefully.

"Sure. If any of you find a functioning vehicle, you may use it!" Jack tells them all.

"Where are we all meeting up?" Conor calmly asked. Dangling from his hook as waits for a reply.

"The other side of the city is where we will meet up. Then we will know of the situation here." Jack informed Conor. Reaching up and grabbing the rope and pulling himself further up.

Climbing the stone wall that has been there for ages. Random spots showing wear. Cracks line certain spots of the wall. In a few crevices there are nest of birds. Different lizards crawling over the wall in search of food. One seems to take an egg from an unguarded nest. Another lizard crawls to near a golem. Which leads it being grabbed and eaten.

The group gets closer to the top. Bright light shines on them from the sun. A few birds rest on the top of the wall. A group of lizards bask in the sun's rays. Hands reaching upward to pull further up the way. Birds fly away as armored hands reach them.

"Ugh. Finally, we made it up here. Can we rest our arms for a bit?" Aiden tiredly asked. Looking down the peak and seeing all landmarks at the bottom.

"Yeah. Only for a little bit. We are burning daylight." Jack answered him.

"It will be easier going down at least." Optimistically spoke Olivia. The others nodded in conjuncture.

The sun hangs over the horizon casting part of the city in light. While the rest is starts to be engulfed in shadow. Parts of the forest start to look ominous. Different animals start to wander under the shade to escape the sun. A pair of uropygid lay down near a tree.

A flock clearmores fly by and land on a patch of grass. The squad of golems start hooking the grapplers onto the side of the wall. Making sure they are secure; they make their descent. Slowly sliding down the rope. They make it a quarter way down before stopping.

Olivia and Jack look around and see how far from the ground they are. *"This should be good enough."* Thought Olivia measuring the distance. "Alright. We can start going faster." Jack let them know.

After hearing that they speed up. Letting their grips loosen they quickly slide down the rope. The ground is fast to approach. Right before hitting the ground, they with haste tighten their grip. Halting their motion, they then jump down. Landing on the ground with a thud.

Glancing around the perimeter to confirm its safety. Once the all-clear is given, they come together. "Ok everyone, get into pairs we are about to check the city." Olivia calmly commands.

The assortment of golems, start to pair up. Olivia is paired up with Jack. Aiden with Liam. And finally, Conor with a purple soldier. With that out the way they all go in different directions of the city.

Jack and Olivia walk through one of the many alleys. Dirt spread out across the street. A knock down trash can down the path. Jack moves a can away with his foot. Puddles of water at different locations on the road. Both seem a little disheartened at the lack of people moving around. However, they understand.

Can't expect people to be walking when there is no one in the city. Fortunately for them there was no blood anywhere. Seems like nothing came this far. No signs of an attack reaching here. Both let out a sigh of relief.

"So far so good. No bloodied corpses or torn limbs." Jack states with relief in his tone. "That should be a good sign." He finishes optimistically.

"True. Let's see if we can find any traces of survivors." Olivia says with a smile. Nodding back to her they start looking for any indication of survivors.

Meanwhile with Liam and Aiden. The mentioned duo seems be having an argument in the street. Both are going back and forth. Liam has an irritated expression. In comparison Aiden is sporting a look of annoyance.

"Would you just drop it already! It would not have made a difference!" Aidan shouts at Liam. Tired of her complaining.

"No, I will not drop it! If those smiths had made those guns and turrets we wouldn't be here!" She shouts back. Confided that it is the smiths' fault.

"They did not have the parts or material to do so. Besides it really wouldn't have changed anything." He rebuked. Feeling tired of this conversation he decides to end it. "Look most of the guns and turrets were for the vehicles. Unless we were going out to meet the enemy, they were going to get over the wall." He stares her down.

"Then let's add the fact we wouldn't have enough wall turrets to halt them." Aiden finishes argument.

"Fine. Whatever, let's just see if there is anything on going here." Retorted Liam upset.

Walking along the street and passing streetlights. The road showing its weathered condition. With many different minor cracks. Many types of buildings line the street. All seeming in good condition and no evidence of struggle. Moving further along they both show their discomfort.

"Still no vehicle huh? Thought we would find one by now." Liam exasperatedly states. Seeing no way of changing that they both continue walking.

Conor and the soldier advance through a neighborhood. Small patches of plants are in front of the houses here. Plain metal fences to keep unwanted guess from entering the area. Luckily nothing seems to have affected them.

"Hmm. Haven't found anybody yet. That could be a good or bad sign." Conor pondered in his mind.

Looking around he spots something in the distance. *"What is that?"* "Hi, lets head over there." He tells his companion. The soldier nods and they both head to the object. Getting a better look, Conor couldn't help but grin.

"Well look at that we found a car." He vocalizes with a joyous mood.

Progressing further Olivia and Jack venture to the other side of the city. Searching around they bear witness to all manner of scattered weapons. There are even random pieces of armor with bites taken out. However, there was a lack of bodies. Still splotches of dried blue and white blood though.

"This is where the conflict most likely ended." Olivia sadly concluded.

"You are likely right." Jack agrees with remorse.

The sound of an engine catches their attention. Turning a car pulls up to them. Not long after a few cars pull up. Coming out of the first car is Conor and the golem soldier. Once everyone got out of the cars, Jack begins to speak.

"I see you all found transportation." He calmly spoke.

"I would say!" A voice says from behind them. Zooming in the location of the voice show Aidan and Liam appearing with the remaining golems. Aidan is the one who spoke. Both Liam and Aidan had a frustrated look on their faces.

"How come they get to find vehicles? We didn't find anything" Aiden said in depression. "I second that. What the hell." Liam mentions in an agreement.

"We just happened to find them." Conor replied. Everybody with a vehicle nodded.

"Let's not focus on that for now. Talking about the lack of bodies is more important." Jack calmly ended the conversation.

Everyone looked around the area and saw that there in fact were no bodies. Just weapons strolled about area. With bits and pieces of armor. After confirming with their own eyes of lack of carcasses. They all crowd around for the discussion that well take place.

"How come there are no bodies? Does that mean they survived?" Liam questioned to the group.

"I would want to believe so, but with all these weapons scattered about I don't think so." Olivia politely stated then added. "Then there is the fact that the pieces of armor that are here have bites taken out of them." She finishes distressed.

"So, we can safely assume that they were probably eaten." Aiden throw his 2 cents in.

"That is probably the likely outcome. If there are survivors hopefully, they can stay safe." Jack spoke "With luck they may return here. Speaking of which there seems to be not threats to the city currently. I think it is safe to call Daiki and have him bring the people here." He states.

"What do you all think?" Jack asks for opinion on the matter.

"I think its ok to call him." Olivia answers.

"Yeah, let the people come back." Aiden says.

"Go for it." Liam adds.

"They should be ready." Conor calmly mentions.

After all confirmations Jack pulls out his military grand phone and calls him. The rest of the squad glance at each other. "So how long do you think it will take them to reach here?" Liam asked curiously.

"Shouldn't take too long. With the vehicles it should only take a few hours." Olivia told her. "That without accounting the random trees. The time could extend if they encountered something to fight something."

"A day max if they are side armed and have to move around." Aiden chimes in. "Things can get really bad if they are unlucky or not carefully."

Deep in the forest there are multiple vehicles in a circle in a minor clearing. Many campfires to keep the residents warm and feed. Some civilians sit around random fires talking amongst themselves. Further away their cattle and other farm animals they managed to bring with them are there grazing.

Everyone here has been in this forest for about a week. All just trying to persevere in these conditions. The golems having been doing well, however. Soon they will hear good news.

"I hope the city will be safe. That way we won't have to start again." Daiki muttered to himself. Daiki is a grass golem that wears black armor. Weapons of choice is a snipe elfir and a bronze color claymore. *If we are really lucky, we will have some survivors from the defenders.* He mulled over.

Hearing a cough Daiki turns to see Tony walking over. Tony plops himself down next to him. Both sit in silence for a few minutes just enjoying each other's company. Tony turns to Daiki to talk to him.

"Is everything alright?" He asked worriedly. The concern showing on his face.

"Yeah, I'm fine. Just tired." He replied with minor bags under his eyes. "I am just hoping that everything is ok in the city. That way we can just bring everyone back and fortify the city."

"I guess see where you are coming from." Tony said understand fully. "I would lov-." Ring! Ring! Ring! He is interrupted by a phone call.

Daiki lifts his hand with his phone up and answered. "Hello?" "The city is safe. Bring everyone here." Jack spoke through the device.

Daiki looks up at Tony with a hopeful expression. "Understood sir. On our way." "Good. See you all later." The phone hangs up.

Daiki goes to the center of the camp. Which gets everyone's attention, exactly what he wants. "Everyone! I have great news! The city is safe to return to! Pack up all the supplies so we can head back!" He made the people aware.

After many cheers and shouts of finally, they start packing up equipment. Daiki heads to the front to make sure everything is going fine. Ten minutes later everyone is ready with civilians in the vehicles with the animals they can fit. With the rest tied to the vehicles so they continue to follow. The soldiers hanging off the back and sides of the vehicles.

The trip starts with the turning of wheels. The driving is a moderate pace. The massive vehicles move through the luscious forest. The twitting of birds and amphibians ring out in the calm atmosphere.

"Keep on this path. If we stay heading in this direction we will get there sooner." Daiki said the driver from the side of the vehicle.

There peaceful drive is about to get rocky. The scale cows start mooing out loud. "Why are they mooing?" Some asked. There question is soon answered. One scale cow is leaped upon by a creature. A guard is then tackled by another.

The creatures seem to be lizard like. Sporting short stubby tails Having deep blue eyes staring menacingly towards their targets. They have a bony exoskeleton with their body being a deep purple.

"Exoskales! Fire!" Someone shouts in distress. Bang! Bang! Bang! Sounds of guns firing echo through the air. Turrets spraying ammo at the attacking menaces.

"Keep them at bay! We cannot allow them to stop us!" Daiki commands the troops.

An exoskale leaps onto the truck that Daiki is on. Quickly swinging his scimitar at the beast. Bisecting it with ease with its parts falling of the truck. Many more exoskales charged the vehicles planning to make a meal out of them. More scale cows were pounced upon. Their collars connected to the transportation ripped apart.

Couple of exoskales leap onto the armored trucks. Bullets through their bodies is their response. Body parts falling to the fast-paced ground. Light purple blood sparkling in the light. Another warrior thrusts his spear into a beast leaping toward him.

"Keep fighting! We must survive!" Daiki commands quickly shooting a creature charging him. "Die you menace."

Whipping his gun in another direction and firing. One exoskale rushes a soldier from behind. Taking her and itself off the vehicle. A person spins a turret firing on ones on the ground. He turns again to shoot in the other direction. Only to come face to face with one of them.

Before he could do anything, it snatches him up. Opening its jaws wide snaps shut onto the golem head. Then all sudden a sword goes through its body. With a quick wretch it is cut in half. Awhile later after a few more golems and cattle die. The exoskales finally give up chase too tired to continue.

"Ah. Its finally over." Someone tiredly says. Many looking exhausted and bloody.

"We lost a few of our siblings in arms. Along with a few cattle. They will be missed." Daiki sadly utters. "But I guess it could have been worse."

Turning his head forward he sees they are not too far away from the city. Its dark shadow casting in the moonlight. He out a sigh of relief knowing its almost over.

Soon they start to approach the gate doors. Pulling up directly in front of the giant doors they come to a stop. Daiki turns his head to look behind to see everyone directly behind him. After checking if they were ready, he pulls out his phone. Turning it on starts calling.

"Hey Jack. We are outside the gates." Daiki calmly informed him. "Good. Opening gates now."

With that said the massive doors started to slide open. After hearing the mechanical click from the doors opening all the way. They drove forward entering the city. Looking up they see a few golems staring down at them. A couple came up them to check their conditions.

"I see that you made it back safe and sound Daiki." Olivia politely said. Walking up to him with the others.

"We lost a few people on the way. Also, some scale cows died." He informed them.

"I see. That explains the marks on the transports." Bluntly stated Liam assessing the damage.

"Anyway, what is happening now? Do you know what happened to the defenders?" Daiki asked them.

"The defenders are most likely dead. All was left were their weapons and bitten into armor." Jack sighs and continues. "For what is happening right now. We are going to make wall turrets. Along with other defenses for the city."

"I see." He said back in an understanding tone.

"Everyone, listen up! Thirty soldiers or so go and help the civilians settle back in. While the rest of us along with the smiths will focus on improving the city's defenses. Is that clear?" Jack commands and asked them. Following their positives, they get to work.

Chapter 16

The group of hikoyasei continue walking through the forest. Grass trampled underfoot. Finished with their resting they are ready to move on. The trees start thinning out making it easier to move. Soon they start hearing noises.

"Hey. What is that sound?" A random hikoyasei questioned.

Nobody said anything not having an answer. Everyone just shakes their heads. Clive just looks up and stated. "Will just have to find out in a bit." He stated calmly. Everyone nodded to that. Felix moved ahead.

"Clive is correct. Let's find out what it is." Felix instructed.

They all arrive further at a clearing. What was causing the commotion was two creatures engaged in conflict. Well, many of one creature trying to consume the other creature. Which seems to be the likely outcome.

The animal that is about to become food seems to be a type of behemoth. A cricket lizard one with four horns. Showcasing shiny bluish scales with a darker exoskeleton. Hooked feet that try to fend of its attackers.

Its assailants seem to be more prepared. One of them swiftly shoots a projectile into the creature's leg. Distracted it wasn't ready to guard itself from one leaping at it. Claws stab through scales rip and tearing which is followed by a deadly bite.

The victors seem to have two sizes and colorations. In general, the beasts seem to be reptilian. Intriguingly one half of them is half the size of the other half. Both sizes have six legs and are sporting two tails. One half seem to have sharp tail tips. With minor exoskeleton armor on their backs. Having a head crest of small spikes. Also being a dull yellow with dusty gray stripes.

Its counterparts have more going on. Not only are they twice the size. They have more tools for disposal. More much sharper and larger teeth.

Longer and sharper claws with small hooks. Instead of singular sharp tips, they have spike club like tips. The exoskeleton seems to cover more of the body. Adding more protection with the scales. The colors on them popping out. With them being a deep yellow carrying black stripes.

Finishing their kill. They start to eat tearing into the behemoth corpse. Blood spilling to the ground. Flesh flying in the air from brutally tearing. Blood-stained teeth entering back into the body.

"What are those!?" Clive exclaimed in a low tone.

"Those are yellow fangs." Felix answered his question. Looking to the hikoyasei all looking at him. "They are a hardy creature. The smaller ones are males."

They nodded following along. "The larger ones are soldiers." He finished. They all look at for further explanation.

"So are the soldier ones genderless?" Clive asked in honest.

"No, they are female, but they don't normally breed." He clarified. "They are the defenders and gathers for the queen yellow fang. The soldiers carry a venomous bite. They kind of work like hive wasps." He added.

"Oh, that makes sense I guess." Someone said absentmindedly

"Anyway, let's move forward. It about time we grab food for the colony." Felix sternly told them.

Everyone quicky nodded and move on. Crawling across the clearing and into a meadow. Making ley way to the massive sized fruit trees. Fully expected creatures to be there as well. That way the get meat and plants for the hikoyasei back home.

Lush trees seem to be occupied by something. Correction multiple somethings are around the trees. Large bird creatures with claws on their wings. All of them standing on all fours.

"Are those thunderbirds?" Clive asked Felix. He who then looked at him and nodded.

"They are indeed thunderbirds." He confirmed as the thunderbirds seemed to have spotted them.

Many proceed to sprint towards them. Talons smoothly move through soil. Other thunderbirds however leaped into the air and started flying. Not letting their opponents wait they moved to rush them as well. Many of the hikoyasei moved to the air as well.

Dirt flying about as feet run over the ground. Small plants stepped on in the pursuit. The once calm air of the forest now ruined. With the plants soon to be feed with blood.

Felix rushes to the opposing thunderbirds. Galloping across the ground feet bouncing about. All the while Clive lead the forces in the air. Arm reared back in preparation to strike. Claws swiping into the beaked face of a purple thunderbird. Blood splattering the ground.

"Back you accursed bird. Die on the ground where you be long." Venomously spoke Felix.

Quickly biting into the neck of it. With a quick turn kills it with a snap. Tossing the body without a second thought. Turning with haste to intercept the two colliding bodies coming towards him.

All three tussling on the ground trying to take out the other. Using his superior strength, he manages to land above them. A hand grasping one of their heads, squeezes crushing the avian head. Claws quickly impales the others throat. With a quick motion he throws a body at another approaching thunderbird.

"Is that the best you-birdies can do!? You aren't even worth my time." Felix shouts with resentment in his voice.

The moon cast a dark shadow overhead. Covering everything below in a pitch-black shade. All of what can be seen of the sky is a dull grey. However, there is a beautiful light. The glow of the blue moon illuminates the sky. Looking like a big gem, the blue moon shines in the sky. Thanks to its light, the battle of two opposing creatures can be seen.

Burning silk is spat at a green thunderbird. It avoids getting hit by doing a barrel roll. All is for naught, as it finishes dodging it is hit with another glob. With one its wings restrained it is unable to fly, and quickly starts falling. Without warning another suffers its fate.

Swiss! A pair of thunderbirds soar towards a hikoyasei. Once in range they both fire sharp sparking feathers. Having no time to veer away the electric charged feathers connect. Electrocuting the large bat as it shrieks in agony. Indignant it retaliates by discharging steaming silk at them both.

Clive swerves out of the way of a beam of lightning. Another crackling beam comes out of the beak of the bird. *That was close. These things are getting a little tricky.* He thought to himself. "Everyone, make sure to take them out quickly! We don't want them charging up!"

The command is answered with nods. With his piece given he continues to fight. *"Also, we don't want to keep the chiefs waiting."* He let out in his head.

Trees are toppled over, the ground with craters in them. Blood and feathers in different places. Clumps of acidic silk on bushes. A corpse here and there. And the song of roaring violence rings in the background.

Bloodied claws wrench free from an avian head. Felix flicks the blood of his hand. Staring down at his paw with disgust. *"These annoyances are getting on my nerves."* He looks over at the battlefield.

Hikoyasei are besting the thunderbirds. Many cadavers of the giant birds were around the area. No lethal causalities for the hikoyasei. The worst they got are a multiple feather punctures or singed fur.

"Well, at least we haven't suffered any losses." He sighed heavily. Just wanting all of this to hurry up.

An orange hikoyasei slams into a blue thunderbird. With excellent precision penetrates the skull of the bird by thrusting it claws. Five thunderbirds are pinned from silk. Three of the giant bats slam into them. Squawks and squeals are let out as blood sprays into the air.

A corpse of an oversized bird falls in front of him. Felix stares for a moment. Turning his head upward and sees how the battle is faring up there. A few more injured hikoyasei here and there. However, no dead.

"Seems Clive has the situation handled. Good." The idea of Clive being one the secondary leaders sounding more appealing. *"Well, let me do my part and finish up here."* He concludes and intercept a charging thunderbird. Grappling the raven looking thunderbird, claws stab through feathers with no resistance.

"Ok, these feathers are agitating." Clive pondered to himself. This aerial battle reminds of those times we he was younger. Him and other hikoyasei would fight owl bears in the sky. While most owlbears can't fly as fast as hikoyasei. They made up for it with a versatile of elements.

Some elements literally made some of the owlbears faster than the hikoyasei. Fire, lightning, air, and water wear the most difficult ones to deal with. Nonetheless, just as they defeated the owlbears. They will conquer these thunderbirds.

Spinning in the air Clive snatches a thunderbird from the sky. Swinging it under him, he insnares its throat with his fangs. Effortlessly crushes the windpipe in seconds. Dropping the carcass, he turns to see everyone else finishing up confrontation. Sighing in relief, he perceives the movement of flapping wings heading towards him.

Just as he is about to rotate, Felix speaks up. "You all did well about here." He commends them. "Was there any doubt?" Clive queries in return. "Nah, just glad you all handled it quickly." Clive nods. "Now let's grab the fruit and the cadavers and we can return."

The swarm of hikoyasei land back onto the ground. Moving in quick succession seize all the fruit carry. Next, they move onto the dead thunderbirds. Each carry two in one hand by the neck they take off back into the sky.

"Wasn't this an eventful day?" Felix asked Clive humorlessly. "It was. We got to see a lot of different things. I even learnt about creatures I wasn't aware of. And what others could do that I did not know."

"Yeah, it was learning experience. Lovely that it is ending with a beautiful night." Felix announced with a small grin.

His remark got multiple nods in return. They all are flying high in the sky ready to return-back to their colony. With hope of getting rest.

Rocky walls of the canyon shine brightly. Light from the moon reflecting off the stone. Bioluminescent moss glowing along the walls. Large shadows filtered over the walls. **Flap! Flap!** The sound of wings following.

The hikoyasei group fly into the tunnels with their spoils. *"Glad to be back."* Felix thought in his mind. Flying ahead they see hikoyasei guarding the tunnels. The guards catch sight of them and shift out of the way.

"How do think everyone is faring? Think they are annoyed that we took so long?" Clive asked an inquiry. "Maybe not. The chiefs might be a bit antsy. We are in new territory and can be killed." Felix replied to him. "Yeah. You are probably right. They would be cautious."

"Well let's hurry up and bring the food. Before they with all intents and purposes become annoyed." Clive inclines his head in agreement.

Finally arriving back to the main chamber, they land. The stream still rushing through with the occasional creature. Many hikoyasei are in the main chamber. With some on the ceiling or the side of the walls. Some munching on large fish. Others seem to be watching crystal spiders crawl upon the walls.

Surveying the area to find a suitable spot. There seems to be a couple of descent spots. They start putting up the food. Hikoyasei from the ceiling fly down to help. Moving food to storage for later, with some of them eating now.

"All right it is time to report." He concluded in his mind. Looking around he finds his leaders on the other side of the boudoir. Vladimir and Tsu'tey seem to be overseeing all of what is happening around them. Felix starts to head towards them to inform them of his report.

"To reasonable results here we go." Felix moves with his line of thinking.

"I see you have returned Felix." Vladimir spoke as he and Tsu'tey turn to face him. "You are ready to inform us of the surrounding area?" He finishes.

"Yes sir. I have a great deal to say." Felix answered determinedly. With how everything is going the need this area to live comfortably. That previous mountain they lived in was their home for decades. Only the older hikoyasei remember living anywhere else. Sure, they are not the only hikoyasei in the world. Nonetheless, only an occasional group joins the flock. As well as only a few leave to start elsewhere. While it is true that not many things can stand against them. With land that can just be taken. There are other creatures of their level that can fight them. That is without them including dragons, goliaths, and limbpexs.

Such territory is unwinnable unless they outnumber them. With certainty they need this land. There are no will competition and plentiful food. Which makes this much worth it.

"There is a variety of food as for example our favorite apples." He continues as he sees both Vladimir and Tsu'tey grinning as they heard this. The pair of them motion for him to go on.

"There are only few creatures that could be a little challenging." "Such as?" Tsu'tey with curiously asked. "We have berserkers, rocs, thunderbirds, and yellow fangs." Was the answer he gave her.

"Are any of the mentioned creatures close? Though only the yellow fangs are dangerous with their numbers." The inquiry was laid out by Vladimir. "No. The yellow fangs' hive are all the way on the other side of the region. I don't know where the other animals live at, but they were far out when they were hunting." Felix replied.

Chapter 17

Large sandy rocks scorching hot from the absorbed heat from the sun. The sun shining in the sky bearing down on the land. Temperatures so high that many different creatures would just burn to death on the rocky surface. That doesn't seem to be a problem for these two creatures fighting. The battle commences between the wyverns and goliaths.

"That's the way!" Oliver exclaims as he smacks a wyvern to the side. Turning around he catches another wyvern trying to slam into him. Grasping the struggling reptile's head, his claws dig in. Following up with no effort tears off its head. Quickly he tosses the decapitated body at an approaching wyvern.

"Gotcha you!" Ilya shouted while leaping over Oliver. Tackling the now downed wyvern with the two of them rolling on the ground. Pining it down she lands on top. Pulling her arms to the sides and she pulls it's wings out of their sockets. **Aah! Aah!** The thing wails in pain. Ilya annoyed by the screeching snaps the things neck shutting it up.

"I see that you are enjoying yourself." Oliver humorously tells her. Moving to face him with a smirk on her face. "Of course, I am. These things don't have a crystal shard catch at beating us. There is no reason not to enjoy ourselves." She retorted with a raised brow.

Well, she isn't wrong. Wyverns in general are no threat to goliaths. The older ones have a better chance. However, the possibilities of them are 2 to 10. Now a group of adults against one goliath might be a different story.

"I guess you are right." He replies turn her. Then while wearing a grin of his own. Both turn to finish off the remaining wyverns on their end.

Scree! A wyvern lets out she bites down on its wing. As Lily is biting into its wing, she nearly severs it in half. Then she throws it away from her. Sunlight glistens off the slime that is on the wyvern. The dark slime glows purple. Such a color was breath taking and attention grabbing. Then it quickly shifted to a bright purple.

Just as the wyvern manages to get to its feet, the slime explodes. Bits of charred bloodied flesh smack into the ground. Lily twirls around with a smirk. Whistling in appreciation of her explosion. The explosion also disorientated some wyverns.

"Now River!" Lily shouted. River moves with immerse speed and proceeds to launch a spike at a falling wyvern. With the spike going into the chest, and it buried into its heart. Nodding to himself in satisfaction he gets ready to continue. Abruptly he extends spikes from his back. Barely seconds later a wyvern charges straight into his back.

Tossing the punctured corpse from his dorsal spikes. Turning around he sees Lily launching a glob of acid at her opponent. **Argh!** The creature lets out in pain.

"That was thrilling. Nice to get the blood pumping every now and again." She thought to herself. Staring down at the melting corpse in gratification. Lily moves her head and glances at River. In tandem both take a glance in the others' direction.

Both are given the honor of watching Oliver kill the last wyvern. The two of them walk over to Oliver and Ilya. "Hu! Looks like we killed all the small ones finally." Oliver breathes out.

"Yeah. I'm ready to get this over with so we can go home. Especially since I am pretty sure our friends are back." Lily spoke up in agreement.

"Speak for yourself barely any of them are my friends. Anyway, blowing things was nice." Ilya said to her with her claws folded.

"Though you must admit it was quaint fun. Don't you think so River?" Oliver mentioned his opinion and then asked River for his. "I will admit it was kind of fun." He let out with a chuckle.

Roar!!!! The adult wyverns roared in fury of all the younglings' demise. "Oh, they didn't like that." Oliver stated as they stared at the enraged parents. Before any of them could reply to his statement, he was slammed into the ground. And then without a moment's notice snatched up into the air.

"Oliver!" Shrieked Ilya in astonishment. "Don't worry! We have your-!" Ilya eyes widened as Lily was grabbed a second later.

Turning over to River she begins her instructions. "Ok you go and help Lily. I will assist Oliver in this battle. Understand?" She informed him. River nodded in agreement.

"Dang I wasn't expecting for them to be snatched up that fast." Ilya thought to herself. *"Oh well. This fight won't be too long. A little challenging though."* She finishes her pondering.

Rushing forward in the direction of Oliver. She sees him in the grasp of a pale gray wyvern. He brandished his claws and stabbed the attacker in its talons. As its grip loosens in pain, Oliver opens his mouth and shoots a projectile into its thigh. In too much pain the wyvern drops him.

Ilya finally catches up. She peers at Oliver looking him over. He had minor lacerations. "I see you caught up. Ready to fight this thing?" Oliver inquired of her with a grin.

She just looks at him then says. "Well, I guess so. Let's get this over with." She vocalized with a minor groan.

The two of them rush forward to combat the wyvern. It flew towards them ready to massacre them. Oliver and Ilya leap up to grapple their larger foe. Claws meet talons and the battle launches into motion.

River sprints over to where Lily was dragged off to. She was currently clawing at the pink wyvern. Tightening its grip on her to prevent her from struggling. That doesn't stop her from secreting slime from her body. Seconds later a small blast burst open the talons. She started to free fall in the air.

Lily stands up from her crouched position. Turning around to see River finally walking up to her. "I see you have made it. Hope you are ready to bring this beast down." Smugly spoke Lily facing him.

"Well, I am ready for this challenge ahead. Though this going to be a little bit hard." He said back to her. The beast screeches at them in angry. With speed rushes towards them. Lily hops out of the way the strike. While River got caught by the tail. Thorny barbs dig into him as he is sent flying. Back hitting the ground forcing air out of his lungs. Turning over he greeted with the sight of Lily trying to hit the thing with globs of acid.

Seeing how she has it distracted, he spits out a ball of sharp barbs at it. The barbs hit the back of the neck. The wyvern buckles for a sec as lets out a pained squeal. Turning to face River, it releases a beam of boiling water at him. By the skin of his teeth, he rolls out the way. Midnight purple slime makes direct contact with one of the wings.

Aah! Aah! Pinky lets out as the slime burns her. Then within a few seconds explodes. The flyer crashes into the ground. Lily tries to capitalize this vulnerability and launches herself at the beast. She is rewarded with a water beam slamming into her chest. Tumbling over the ground from the hit. She starts to dry heave air knocked right out her.

Ilya flings slime at the gray wyvern. The slime misses and the beast twirls in the air. It then quickly slams into her, knocking her to the ground. Before further harm could happen to Ilya, Oliver fires bullets from his arms into the creature. Recoiling from being shot, it turns to Oliver in angry. Firing a breath of ash towards him. He quickly ducks under the beam.

Ilya quickly gets revenge by jumping onto the wyvern. Fangs sinking into its thigh. The reptile shrieks and tries to shake her off. Oliver takes a page from Ilya's book and attacks the other leg. Ilya starts to coat the scales in ooze. She leaps back as the explosion hits the beast. Then follows up with skin specks throw at its feet. The following explosion topples it over.

Hitting the ground gray shakes its head to get the dizziness out. Oliver starts blasting the wyvern adding to the pain. In a blink of an eye, it grabs Oliver in its jaws. Biting down, crushing Oliver in its mouth. "Aah!" Ilya moves forward and decks the beast in the face causing an explosion. Releasing Oliver as it roars in pain.

"Oliver are you ok?" Ilya asked in concern. Oliver on the ground with bite marks on him. Struggling to get up he manages to get on his feet. "Yeah. I am fine. Hurt though." Oliver replied to her.

Roar! Both of their attention was grabbed by the roar. Sighing Oliver morphs his right arm into a gun shape. "Lets back to fighting this thing." Ilya nods and coats her arm in fluid and loose bumping skin. "Yeah. Let's do this!"

Oliver and Ilya go to attack their adversary. She goes to try to punch and claw. While Oliver starts firing from the distance pining it down.

A blast of water rams into River's shoulder. Sending him tumbling to the ground. River flips over right before a clawed foot stomps in the location he was just in. Before the wyvern could press the attack Lily spits slime onto the wyvern's foot. Trying to lift its foot pink found resistance as the slime stuck its foot to the ground.

Right as the wyvern was trying to move the foot again, River stabbed it with extended spikes from his arms. **Shriek! Howl!** Pink let out in agony. Moving an arm, he impales its shoulder. The angry lizard having enough of this, clamps onto his arm. "Aah!" He let as was thrown the air. Lily tried to retaliate only to be seized in pink's jaws. "Argh!" She lets out as the wyvern starts to crush her body.

Before it could do too much damage, she oozed out slime. Burning slime started scorching its mouth. A blast soon followed forcing it to let go of the goliath. Sooner than she could move a tail sailed and slammed into her. Pink finally yanks it foot out of the sticky slime and takes of into the air.

River moves to his feet and looks up. Seeing the wyvern preparing to release a beam of water he starts running. Operating on all fours he dodges the beam aiming at him. Out the corner of his eye he sees Lily doing the same as him.

"We are going to have to find a way to get back on the ground. If this keeps up, we will get exhausted first." She says to him. Jumping over debris she turns her head back towards.

"Yeah. And once we do we need to clip its wings show it won't fly again." He told as scattered rocks nearly hit him.

Roar! Pink has beams of water fire from the claws of its wings. Now they need to watch out for more than one beam at time. The pair of goliaths throw the occasional rock at pinky. The game of cat and mouse continues.

Creatures as a whole no matter what, have always had advantages over each other. Whether it was size, speed, numbers, arms, venom. Animals of the sky have two advantages over land creatures. One being the ability to fly and the other being stamina. The draw back was a more fragile body. With it a major weak spot.

"Take out its wings!" Oliver shouted with the top of his lungs. Firing at the airborne reptile. Whom in turn avoids all the shots by bolting out of the way of the bullets.

"Easier said than done!" She yells back. Picking up a stone she covers it in powder from her skin. Lining up a shot she hurls it at grey. A blast of ash hits the rock causing an explosion.

"Damnit!" She hisses in frustration. Grey opens its mouth and releases a ray of ash towards her. She answers in kind, spitting out a ball of explosive material.

The ball connects with the beam causing a blinding explosion. With the wyvern unable to see, Oliver takes this chance. Firing into one of the wings. It buckles but doesn't fall out the sky. However, it is low enough to leap on. Oliver turns to Ilya.

"Ilya! I am going to throw you to it!" Oliver said to her. She looks back and nodded. Rushing towards him she jumps into his claws. "Now!" She shouts. He tosses her into the air. Using her blast ability, she flies straight to their adversary.

"I am on!" She states as she grabs the wyvern. Climbing to its back she reaches the shoulders. Grey tries to shake her off. Ilya starts biting and scratching grey's wings. Then goes to punching it with explosive fists. While doing damage it is not enough.

"Oliver! I am about to cover it with blast powder." Ilya informs her friend. Oliver looks up and nods. Ilya starts secreting fluid and dead skin. Having it leak all over the beast covering its wings and sides. "Now!" She shouted. "Got it!" He aims and fires hitting a spot near the wings. Ilya jumps off right before the shot connects.

Once the bullet makes contact an explosion happens. The huge explosion engulfs the wyvern. For a brief, moment it looked like a phoenix. No longer capable of flying grey crashes to the ground. Causing a crater to form beneath it.

Mewl! Mewl! It lets out in laboring breaths. Bloodied and beaten it lays on the ground. Many burn marks over its body with missing scales in some parts. Oliver and Ilya slowly start walking towards the defeated foe. As the lets out another pained moan, they arrive upon it.

"Well, time to get this over with." Oliver said as he rotates his gun morphed arm towards its head. Pressing the tip against the wyvern's head he fires. **Bang!** He pulls his arm back. Blood spilling from the large hole in the corpse's dome.

"Well, that's done." Ilya spoke up peering at the cadaver. "Even with it being challenging at the end there. Still was an enjoyable battle." She finishes with a grin.

"I guess you are right. This was enjoyable." He responds carrying a smirk. "Plus, it is nice to use abilities we don't use often. Speaking of which why didn't you use your blaster ability?" He asked curiously.

"That is because it was moving too much. My shots are not as accurate as yours." She answers his question.

"I guess that makes sense." He nods his head in comprehension. Walking up to her nods his head in the other's direction. "Think they will need help?"

A water blast is dodged by Lily. Grabbing random rocks, she coats them in slime and makes a club whip like weapon. Swinging the whip, she tries to strike their opponent's leg. Yet, pink was just out of reach. Tsking in annoyance, Lily attempts something else.

"This bastard really won't come down." She mutters with venom. Inching her head to the side she sees River morphing his left arm.

Massive spikes are erected from the arm. With the hand is now barreled shaped. "This should get it out the sky." He says with a determined tone.

Then he starts rapidly firing at the wyvern. A few shots hit dead center and damages the thighs. While other shots just graze the beast. Incensed it aims the tips of its wings and fires upon River. He doesn't have time to escape the assault. The bombardment pushes him into the ground. Which then the wyvern releases its breath on top of him.

"River! Are you alright!" Lily shouts to him. He slowly gets up and lets out a huff. "Yes, I am ok. I just want this over with." River calls back a little vexed.

"Ok. Let's finish this." She confidently states right before reforming the slime. The slime takes the shape of a bow. Rock and slime both to harden the base. She then mixes rock and slime to make a pointed arrow.

Bow in one of her claws and with the string in the other see takes aim. Carefully arranging the shot in the direction of the wings. Pulling the string with great force. Without further issue releases the string. Shoring through the air with unimaginable speeds, the arrow punctures one wings from the shoulder.

Aah! Shriek! Pink screeches out as it falls below in agonizing pain. Acid from the slime eating through the forearm. The heavy body slams into the ground cracking it.

"Finally, we got it out the sky!" Lily says in exasperation. River shakes his head in complete agreement. "Let's make sure it doesn't get back up." He states as he shoots one its legs.

Aah! The pink wyvern bellows at the further affliction. Its injured wing and accompanied with the wounds on its legs it could not get back up. Lily creates another weapon. Walking forward she plunges a slime spear through its head. The slime then liquefies and starts melting the head.

"Well, that is a mission done." A voice says to them. Both turn around to spot Oliver and Ilya strolling over to them. Both sporting grins.

"And we were congratulated by Calmar and Claire. Which brings us too here." Oliver finishes their tale.

"I got admit that sounded awesome." Solar voices with his eyes gleaming. Oliver and his group turn to see everyone inclining their heads in accordance.

"Though it sounded like you struggled more than anyone Ilya!" Helga speaks in a patronizing voice.

"Bitch I know you aren't talking-!" She is interrupted by a commotion from above them. **Roar! Roar! Roar!** Sounds of howls and roars echo from the surface. Silence fills the whole room. They look at each other in mild confusion.

"What was that?" Was the question inquired by Dawn. However, no one could answer her.

Chapter 18

Throughout history creatures have evolved many ways to survive. Or just to get by in life. Many things are different today then what they were in the past. Two tools weren't an option back then. The ability to harness elements and weapons of creation. Even ancient creatures such as dragons, goliaths, and limbpexes were included in this.

Back in prehistoric times no creature had any elemental ability. Even the first dragons. Prehistoric dragons like anything else had to use their physical abilities. The only skills that could be used for long range was spikes if the dragon had any. The prehistoric dragons that had other talents used poison, venom, acid, or even the sound they produce.

It was the same for the goliaths and limbpexes. However, unlike their modern-day counterparts. The uses weren't as versatile. Sound attacks was no different than roaring loudly. Acid could only be spat at a target. Venom had to come from fangs or a stinger whether it was injected or sprayed. Poison had to be ingested which normally meant bitten into.

They could not manipulate their or outside material. They did not have that much resistance to being attack by the substance they used. Meaning an acid dragon can succumb to acid. Or a poison goliath dying to poison. Times back in the prehistoric era were much tougher.

Nonetheless, evolution hit its peak. Many creatures started developing elements and resistances. Which in turn made them more powerful. Intelligence in many organisms grew higher. That's when the creation and use of tools started. Animals that could use elements formed weapons, armor, or other tools from their element.

While those that didn't have elements use the environment around them to make tools. Creating different types of weapons, defenses, and ways to get food. Golems are one such species.

Clank! Clank! The sound of metal hitting rock resounded in the small cave. Inside the cave, dim purple light fills the room. The light coming from crystals on the ceiling. A group of golems are in the process of mining ore. Large pickaxes in their hands. Slamming pickaxes into rocks, small sparks coming off. **Clank! Clank! Clank!** The melody of mining spreads across the room.

Their leader of this assignment is across the room watching them. Daiki nods his head in satisfaction with what they have done so far. The overseer steps towards them all. Looking around to make sure he has their attention. All the noise of mining temporally stops.

Once he sees that they are all paying attention he starts. "Remember! We must collect as much metal ore as possible. The people need us to succeed in getting this resource. With more metal there will better defenses for the city which ensures the people's safety." Daiki firmly reminds them.

Riiinng! Riiinng! Ring! Daiki's phone rings grabbing his attention. "Continue with you all's work. That is all." He tells them. They start to get back to work. The sound pickaxes hitting rock starts back up. Picking up his phone he answers it.

"Hello?" Daiki calls out in greeting. "How is the operation going?" A voice says from the other side of the line. "Ah. It is going well Jack. We almost have all the ore here. There is nothing to worry about sir." Jack is informed by him.

"Jack. Tell him that once they are done, they all can come back. That should be enough ore for now." Aidan muffled voice is heard. "Alright Aidan. So, I am pretty sure you heard him. Come straight back once you all are done." He instructed him. "Yes sir. I will make we will." The phone is hanged up.

He goes to inform the others once they are finish, they are heading back the city. However, he is stopped by a sound. The noise is coming from outside, with that in mind he goes to investigate. Heading to where he heard the sound, the culprit shows itself. Daiki is greeted to the sight of a battalion of trolls marching forward.

Seeing what they are up against Daiki calls for the others. "Everyone, come out here! And be prepared! We might have trouble." He tells them. After hearing him call them, they step out of the cave. Weapons in hand.

Now with the whole golem squad it may not be that hard. The enemy combatants don't aren't as advanced as them. Equip of the marching trolls varies. Which consist of bone armor, leather armor, or metal armor for defense. For the assortment of weapons goes from bone spears to metal swords.

Indefinitely the golems equip is superior. In other words, it wouldn't hold up against their claymores and never their guns. Nevertheless, the trolls outnumber the golems which could pose a problem. Daiki holds up his hand to hold his man back from firing. He then faces the trolls and calls out to them.

"What brings you all here?" He asks them politely. A troll in the lead speaks up. "We are here to take all of your possessions." He said in a matter-of-fact tone.

"Well, we can't have that. Is there not some agreement that can be meet between us." Daiki says in between clenched teeth and his eyes narrowed. "No! We are going to kill all of you and take your possessions!" The lead troll spat out at them. Seeing no way for a compromise he allows his men to start firing.

Bang! Bang! Bang! Soldiers start taking shots at the troll hoard. Bullets going completely into the makeshift armor and out of the body.

They start mowing down the trolls. However, many reach them. And close-range fights start to happen. Though in the current moment it made little difference. Not only are the golems a few feet taller than trolls, but they are also bulker. Even without weapons and armor, trolls wouldn't be able to beat golems.

Golems have much sharper teeth and along with sharper claws. While trolls have a higher bite force, their teeth wouldn't be able to properly puncture their skin. Troll skin is barely tougher than bear hide. While a golem's skin is more akin to armor. It would take about 20 trolls to take out a single golem.

While that may not be the case here. The odds haven't really changed. With the trolls having mediocre equipment and the golems more advanced weapons it is understandable. Bone clubs bounce off tough armor. Tridents skewering trolls with ease.

"As long as we stay on top of them, we have nothing to fear!" Daiki shouts to them all. Twisting his body to bisect a charging foe. Flinging the blood from his blade.

Minutes go by as the fighting continues. Weak metal axes fall to even scratch titanium armor. Large scimitars slice through standard metal swords. A green golem decapitates a grey troll. Its head flying in the blood trickling to ground.

Victory may be on the side of the golems, but the trolls are making much harder for them. Boxing them in certain stabs start getting through gabs in the armor. So far none of the golems have fallen, but wounds will eventually stack up. It is only matter of time. Many were already groaning from stab wounds.

Right before any golem could die an engine is heard. An armored vehicle drives up to the skirmish. "Looks like we made it in time. We got you all covered." Spoke a golem on the turret of the vehicle. Spinning the gun around she starts firing.

Bullets moving at rapid speeds shred the makeshift armor with ease. All that could be seen was bullets going in one way and out the other. The trolls that are being fired upon are hiding behind trees and rocks. Some trying to shoot arrows at the vehicle. "Kill that golem! We can not fall here-!" He is interrupted by screeches.

The whole area goes quiet, no one firing weapons. More screeches are heard as they cut through the silence. It seems that the sound is originating from behind the trolls. Who all turn around to see what it is. Which doesn't take long to find out. Dark quill fuzz claws rush into the area.

Dozens of them come charging for them. Trolls try to fight back and kill them. They didn't a chance. "Aah!" Bloodied screams ring out as trolls are torn to pieces. Within seconds the remaining trolls are killed. However, it seems golems are on the menu too.

"Fire and retreat!" Daiki screams towards them as he fires upon the charging forces.

The armored vehicle attempts to drive off. But it doesn't get far as the little demons jump onto it. Bullets fly free from the turret as she tries to get them off the vehicle. Dark quill teeth rip though armor and flesh leaving nothing left. Those in the truck are killed shortly after.

Daiki and the others start running faster. No matter how fast they run they can escape. One by one they are caught and eaten. Daiki strains himself to get them off him. His limbs are removed along with it his life. No one was left in the forest.

The great walls of the golem city stand proud and tall. Of course, the wall has went through some changes. Now adoring on top of them are many turrets. Currently standing atop of the wall is a pair of golems. Jack seems to be in distress as he attempts to call someone on his phone.

"This isn't good, Liam. Daiki hasn't been responding. And last we spoke he and his team was about to the mission." Jack turns to face her with a troubled look.

"Well maybe they are handling something, and he can't answer." Responding to him with a calm tone. Liam then shrugs showing there isn't that much they can do.

"That may very well be the case. Which doesn't paint a pretty picture." He remarks in a dark undertone. Their conversation is interrupted by chants. Both turn their heads to see what is happening.

A small army of trolls are marching to the city's walls. Hoots and shouts about how they were to conquer the city. Even from here they could hear laughter coming from the forces. Won't be long now. Of course, they weren't the only ones to hear the ruckus.

Olivia, Aidan, and Conor walked straight up to them. Many others on the walls were staring at the approaching army. You could see the disbelief in their eyes. The trolls' actions don't make any sense. It is like they want to die.

"Are they stupid? Do they really believe they can breach the walls. That would never happen. Not with those primitive weapons" Aiden said incredulously.

Arrows are repelled by the walls as they are fired. The army doesn't even make it halfway to the foundation before the start being shot. Automatic turrets fire hot lead into the masses. The few non automatic turrets are used as well.

Trolls start to rush forward to attack the wall. The army barely makes any leeway. Jack and his teammates just shake their heads at the trolls' actions. What did the trolls expect? *"Not the brightest ones, are they?"* Conor contemplates to himself.

"They are like a starfish trying to bite into a rock." Aidan speaks with an eyeroll.

"This fruitless endeavor should end in 10 minutes." Said Olivia in exasperation. "I can't believe that they are really attacking us." Liam adds her two cents.

"Well, we could only wait until it is over" Jack said with a sigh. All of them watch more trolls die.

Archers try to hit the turrets with their arrows. None connect because they can't go that high or are blown up. More troll bodies burst in fleshly bits. One troll loses his leg then arm, then head. Another loses her whole cavity.

Shrieks tore through the air, startling everyone. The turrets stop firing and everyone looks up to see dark fuzz claws. Amass of the pale two-legged creatures with their dark spikes glistening in the light. The trolls try to mount a defense. It was for naught, however.

Trolls were slaughtered in the dozens. Nothing mattered to the beasts. One being stabbed by a troll only allowed for others kill it. They tried everything to stay alive. Their weapons and armor were useless. Where there were once trolls, now aren't any.

Turrets started firing to halt the menaces. The creatures were fast and numerous. Quill claws were already upon the wall. Soldiers firing down to kill as much as possible.

"Get everyone into the buildings now!" Jack ordered as they fired onto the mass. Noticing how little that did he came to decision. "Retreat! Into the buildings!" He shouted as they start jumping from the wall.

The noise of the turrets still firing didn't make them fill at ease. Because not to long after they jumped from the walls the creatures was at the top. Luckily the citizens were inside shelter. Mini beasts jumped down after them. A few golems began shooting them. They didn't last long as they were leaped upon.

"Quick into that building!" Jack said after witnessing the massacre. They all run inside and slam the door. And not a moment too soon. Dark quills scratch at the door.

Many more are attacking the doors and windows. Fortunately for them, they hold. Their building isn't the only one being attacked. Luckily it seems everyone is safe. The creatures stop and start to walk around. Rather aimlessly.

"Why are dark quills back? Did they come to finish us?" Liam says with her heart racing.

"No. I don't believe so. This attack is different." Aidan spoke after catching his breath.

"What do you mean by that?" Olivia politely asked. Aidan turns to look at them." I mean these ones are acting different. This whole is not the same as the last one. Think about it." He says staring at them.

"He is right. They were focused on the trolls first then attacked us." Jack spoke up and sees what Aidan getting at. "There are no variants of them out there. Plus, they didn't evolve from eating like the random ones we saw."

"That is right, when we saw dark quills while on missions, there were different types." Conor joined the conversation. "I remember how shocked we were, when a spider one developed wings from eating a bird."

"Exactly. There is only one type here. And no form of organization. They aren't acting like wolves or a pack. While we seen many without an alpha. They are normally around. Which means these ones are independent." Jack stated.

"Though I am not sure if that is a good thing or a bad thing." Sense they are attacking like a locust swarm." Aidan hops right back in.

"Well, we will have to wait and see. At least they seem too weak to break inside." Olivia tiredly says.

Everyone stares outside the window. About thirty minutes later the dark quills seem to give up and leave. Some time went by before anyone went to check. Nonetheless, they did in fact leave.

"Oh! Thank goodness." A random person muttered. Everyone starts to go back to what they were doing. Jack had a small meeting with the others.

"We need something that can deal with them. A better defense specifically for them." He said to the others. Aidan rose his hand. "I am thinking something with fire."

Chapter 19

There are many great things about the forests of the planet. Not just the forests, but the rest of the biomes of naviros. One moment there can be massive trees. Next moment you could be entering a large lake. Heck sometimes there are fields.

A familiar group of dragons, transverse the current landscape. Moving along the trees' edge and into the meadow side. In different areas rock crawlers move about. With some even drilling into the soil. The group are examining the borders edge.

"I don't see any traces of dark quills here. I do not think any came through here." Roy calmy states.

Glancing about but not seeing any tell signs. No markings, no died remains, nothing. Hydra shrugs at this information. Not really caring too much. If there are none here, fine. When there are some dark quills, he will erase them from existence.

Tom nods his head in conjuncture to his comment. Jim narrows his eyes in irritation. Turning to stare at Roy with a look of anger. "They could just be further out. Did not think off that." He comments aggressively.

"Or did you think everything is a game." Jim snapped at Roy. Who looked back with a look of annoyance. "You are one talk! Always missing up because you don't check for things needed." He shot back.

"Both of you cease this nonsense! This is not the time for your games!" Tom commanded them both. Right before they could continue arguing the sound of flapping wings reached their ears.

All four of them turned their heads to the source. Three dragons land not too far away from them.

Each one of the dragons were full grown. Not old dragons like Tom or Scourge, but they were adults. The first one was a tannish orange dragon.

Another was a lime green color, licking his lips. The final one, who seems to be the leader of the trio. Had midnight black scales adorning his body.

"Who are dragons? And why are you here near the territory of our mountain?" Tom sternly interrogated the foreign dragons. Our group of four staring them in suspension.

The dragons just snicker at them. With the black dragon moving to speak. "I do not believe that is you all's concern." He arrogantly spoke. Shaking his head in amusement.

"Now listen here. You are trespassing in our territory. So, unless you are here to prove yourselves and join us. I suggest you all leave." He told them with a dead serious tone.

"Yeah. I think we have something else in mind." Dragon with black scales said with a grin.

Before they could ponder over what he meant, green moved. Acid was sprayed from the green dragon. The target was Roy who didn't have time to dodge. It eclipses his whole body with falling to the ground. "Aah! Aah-!" he barely has a chance to scream. His body melts down into a bubbling puddle on the forest floor.

"Roy! You bastards will pay!" Tom mourned the death of his disciple. *"How could this happen."* He thought to himself.

Faster than any of them could react. Hydra is attacked. The black dragon slams into him. His larger body easily carrying away Hydra's smaller frame. Claws digging his body as he struggles. Hydra was brought to one side.

Tom having enough of this, acts. He tackles the orange dragon. Both slamming into the ground. Both swiping at each other. Claws leaving gashes across scales. In rage Jim flies into the acid dragon.

Wanting revenge for his fallen teammate, he goes for the attack. His smaller body barely pushes the larger body. Green slams Jim into the ground. Right before he could attempt to crush him. Jim bites into his wrists. "Aah!" He screams and snatches his arm back in pain. Swinging his tail to prevent Jim from getting a follow up attack.

Jim tumbles across the ground from the hit. Quickly getting up he launches back to the acid dragon. Raking his claws along his body. Leaving trails on greenie's body blood leaking from the wound. Roaring in anger green turns his head towards Jim.

Opening his mouth with a large ball of acid forming. Acid is sprayed at Jim. Fortunately for him, he was able to dodge in time. Seeing an opportunity Jim releases his own breath attack. However, it only grazed him.

Tom punches orange across his head. Orange crashes into the ground. Getting up without pause, he fires of a breath attack. A beam of sparks came out. They pounce, happily of his scales. Rearing up his tail he swings it right into his adversary's side. The club from his tail leaving an indent in his sides.

Hydra's back hits the ground as the black dragon pins him. Opening his mouth, he spews ice at his foe. "Rah!" He lets out as frost covers his face. Stumbling back and off Hydra. Hydra his tail in a striking motion preparing to jab him. Following through with the motion he stabs the black dragon's shoulder.

"Aah! You little bastard! You will pay for that!" He all but roars at Hydra. Pissed that he has been hit twice now.

"Try it bitch!" He fired back in an icy tone. Immediately he has no choice but to eat his words.

As fast as lightning he is slashed across the chest. Before he could let a scream, black grabs him by the neck. Moving on his back legs, lifts Hydra from ground. And in quick motion throws Hydras through some trees. Hydra struggles to catch his bearings.

"Dawn that was fast. Didn't even see him move either." He thought inside his mind. Completely shocked at how fast the adult dragon was. Shaking his head to reorient himself.

Strolling between the broken trees the older dragon glares down at him. "Caught you didn't I." The smoke dragon grumbled out. Jaws widening as a beam of smoke comes out.

Jim covers his tail in ash and tries to club the acid dragon. Who dodges to the right of the attack. The tail cratering the ground beneath. Green covers his claws in acid, lunges forward to Jim. Forming ash over his wings to block the attack. Pointing his wings to his opponent he fires the ash at him.

"Try that for size!" He exclaimed as his attack hits dead on. Quickly forming ash around himself he blasts off towards green. Ramming into his side making him gasp for air.

"I am going to enjoy killing you." Green venomously says after recovering from the strike.

His stony club tail smacks into the smaller dragon's head. Going for a strike towards his opponent's head, he misses. Orange rolled out of the way in a nick of time. Holding his head to help himself recover. Turning he glares at Tom. Gripping the ground, he shot towards him. Slamming right into him. Seizes this chance he fires a beam point blank at Tom chest.

Clancy and the others race up to the surface. Rushing through all the tunnels to get to get topside. Making it to the entrance, they come out into the moon's light. Once there on the surface he looks around. Spotting many other elder and adult goliaths. Glancing over he sees that the younger goliaths are there too.

"What is happening?" Clancy thought to himself. *"What could have made those roars?"* He continued thinking.

Turning his head to see what his colleagues' thoughts were. Unfortunately, they had the same confused expressions as he did. However, the answer to everyone's questions is about to be answered.

With the moon brightly shining through the darkness, they can see through the darkness clearly. What they see is creatures being caste in the light of the moon. A hoard of them to be exact. Dark quills of different types and sizes. With there being three variants of hunter.

For the hunter variants there was the behemoth type that was mixed with some kujira traits. Another was type was the krypto with scorpion like tails. The final hunter type had the base of a hybodus with characteristics of a beetle. Some being half the size of the younger goliaths. While others were about the size of the adolescents.

Then we have the alpha dark quills as well. Of course, with four variants. A few uropygid base ones with traces of siderops and troll. Koatl variants mixed with barb claws and blood hyenas. Next version being berserkers having DNA of golems and rippers. With the last alpha type being moth rays having spider and crab characteristics. All of them sizing to the adult goliath's height.

And leading it all a dark quill with a human appearance. Thorny hair reaching his shoulders. The spikes pointing down on his back like a shell. Worn out robe over his body. A mischievous grin on his face.

"Time for these beasts to fall for the glory of White spine." Ren said to himself in a whisper. Pale hair in motion thanks to night breezes. He has this assault well. Building up his troops and increasing their strength from all the different creatures around.

"What are those things? What type of creatures are these?" Solar asked out loud. No one could answer him though. None knowing the answer themselves.

"The time is now. Go forth my brethren and kill them all! Dark quills do not leave any single one alive! Take all the DNA you can!" He commanded.

Thousands of hunters and alphas charge forwards to the hundreds of opposing goliaths. "Well, there is your answer." Chloe said to Solar who just looked at her. The goliaths prepare themselves. The two forces clash.

A goliath grabs a hunter by the neck and stomps down on another. An alpha and a pair of hunters pin a goliath down and ends its life. One group of hunters is hit with a ball of fire. All of them being incinerated. In another area an alpha is ripped in half.

Clancy is accosted by a pair of alphas. One being a uropygid and the other being a berserker. Fanged mandibles clamp down onto his arm. "Aah!" He lets out in minor pain. Before the other could hit him with its claws, he moves. Slamming the one on his arm into the other.

Dazed its mandibles release its hold on him. Not missing the opportunity, he grabs the dark quill's mandibles. Pulling his arms in opposite directions. Clancy tears the beast in half. Blue guts and blood falling to the floor. An obsidian blade extends from Clancy's wrist and into the alpha trying get up.

"And stay down." He said right before a group of hunters came rushing froward.

"Well, here we go." Spin-ray calmly says as she combats the enemy. Claws decapitating a trio of hunters. She shoots a cactus needle at a dark quill attacking another goliath. Who nods his head in appreciation. With a twirl she slams her tail against a hybodus hunter trying to get the jump on her.

"It is not going be that easy to beat me." She says taunting the dark quills. Angered by here demeaner three alphas charge her. A koatl alpha lunges towards her. Spin-ray extends a cactus blade from her arm and stabs the alpha. Staring at it struggles she heaves the blade in an upward motion.

The nearly bisected corpse falls to the ground. Leaving its blue blood on the blade. Immediately Spin-ray impales the second one through its head. Effortlessly swings the alpha into its compatriot. Causing it to tumble to the ground.

Removing her blade from the dead one, she marches forward. Swinging her arm, she severs the last one's head. Looking at her arm blade, her face scrunches up in disgust. Oscillating her arm to get the blood.

"Well, that was that." She mutters emotionless. "Time to kill some more."

One purple goliath is currently pummeling a berserker dark quill. Caving in its chest and head. She gets up from her kill. Only for her to have her neck grabbed by a dark quill uropygid. Squeezing down on her neck crushing her windpipe. As it starts to eat it is interrupted.

"Oh, we can't have that now can we." A feminine voice stated. Right before it could move a clawed hand emerges from its chest. It falls over dead.

Chloe brings her bloodied claw to her mouth and licks it. Smacking her lips as she does so. Putting a finger to her lip as she thinks. Then she puts her hand down and shrugs. "Tasted alright." She spoke.

Gyrating her head, she sees a group of 4 coming straight to her. The dark quills hunger for flesh and blood. Releasing a sigh, she morphs her hand in a multi barrel gun. Rat-tat-tat! Rat-tat-tat! Rat-tat-tat! Chloe fires with the speed of a minigun.

The group is decimated. They could get any closer before their bodies were shredded. Their corpses painting the landscape blue. She just shakes her head. Pivoting her cranium upward to stare the moon.

"Tonight, is beautiful night." She says with a little laugh. "And about to get better." She let a smirk as stared at an alpha type.

Crashing into an alpha, Solar grabs the creature skull. Claws tearing into it he rips it off. Letting the body fall to the ground. Spinning he rakes his claws across a hunter's body. He proceeds to grab it and spits a boiling substance in its face. The beasts head started to melt.

Turning he catches a leaping krypto dark quill. Solar holds it in place as he burns it alive in his hands. Steam visibly coming off him. Dropping the corpse, he sees a group trying to ambush him. Solar propels himself over the group of hunters. Once directly above them he spits out some boiling liquid.

They fall to the ground screaming in agony. Then out of nowhere an alpha tackles him. Both grapple on the ground. Grabbing its jaws, Solar starts wrenching it open. With a show of force rips the jaws off. Crushing its skull to finish it.

Chapter 20

"Prepare to die, boy!" Roared the black dragon. Blasting smoke directly at Hydra. He attempts to get out of the way but is grazed on his left side. "Aah!" Letting out a pained groan as he looks at his opponent. Only to see him going for another attack. Hydra rolls away as the black dragon tries to impale with his tail.

Hopping up from the grassy ground to proceed in his battle. Turning with a flap of his wings, he charges towards the smoke dragon. "I don't know who you are calling boy. However, underestimating me is a sure fine way to get killed." He spoke with a frosty tone.

"I don't a youngling like you could hurt me. The mighty Miles." He said in a cocky tone. Hydra rams into the larger dragon's chest. For a moment stunning him. That is enough time to claw his chest and blast him with ice. "Argh!" Quickly hitting Hydra away, moves his claw to his chest.

Pulling his hand away to blood covering his palm. Turning his to glare at Hydra. Miles's face scrunches up in anger. If looks could kill, Hydra would be dead a hundred times. Tossing the blood from his paw, he growls at Hydra.

"Don't start getting cocky boy. I am still not even really trying." Miles said to Hydra with annoyance.

"We will see about that." Hydra flies above him then drops. Spinning as he falls. All but shoving Miles into the ground. Clawing at his back Miles covers himself in smoke.

Hands burnt from the smoke causes Hydra to recoil in pain. Next, he knows he is hit with a tail sending to the earth below. Hydra shifts to the right barely avoiding a foot. A crater forming with he was just at. In a furl of motion goes under Miles and starts biting his legs.

The orange dragon tosses a ball of hot sparks at Tom. Shifting his hand into a club, he smacks the ball away. Irritated with his attacks being causally being rebuffed, he attacks. Covering his body in crackling sparks. Planning to tackle the slighter larger dragon. Tom strikes the smaller spark dragon across the face. Halting his charge and hurting him. Bloody gashes are there from Tom's claws.

"Ugh! Urgh!" He groans grabbing his face. Looking though his blood caked hands. He sees Tom calmly standing there with no signs of worry. This infuriates him, none of his attacks have been working. Time, he changed that.

"I have had enough of you. Fighting against me like you stand a chance. Prepare to join the ancestors!" Sparky shouts as flaps his wings lifting himself up in the air.

"This will teach him." He thought infuriated with the stone dragon. Getting an optimal height, he flares up. Glowing embers coming off his body. Scales now a bright illuminate orange. He stares down at Tom in contempt. Then starts spreading his wings.

"Time to die! At least you get to see that purple dragon again!" Laughing at memory of Roy's death. The spark dragon storms towards the older dragon. Crashing into him with all his weight. This does not even effect Tom. He was only moved a few inches. The sparks aren't even hot enough to burn him.

Not dissuaded he goes for a follow up attack. Opening his jaws wide he bites Tom's shoulder. Still his attacks are ineffective as his teeth couldn't penetrate his stony hide. Also, his teeth were too weak to handle the pressure and broke. Recoiling from the pain in his mouth.

Tom looks down at the smaller dragon. A cold expression on his face. Walking forward with a snarl he smacks his opponent with his tail. He grabs him by his neck and lifts him up to his face.

"How dare you come to our domain and kill one of our own!" Tom snarled. Staring directly in his eyes. Then a smirk appeared on his face. *"This bastard has the gull to smirk. I am going to enjoy killing him."* He thought with fury.

"It was easy. Not our fault he was very weak." Sparky chuckled to himself. "Besides, you all don't deserve this land." He finished.

Before Tom could crush his neck, he blasted him with embers. Taking off into sky to escape. Tom quickly follows right after him. Releasing a torrent of liquid stone at the orange dragon. His blast manages to connect with him. "Aah!" He screams as he plummets to the ground.

His wing shredded, there nothing he could do to slow his fall. Colliding with the ground leaves him with broken bones and lacerations. Tom lands right beside him. He positions his hand over the incapacitated dragon's body. Pinning him to the ground for him to finish him off. Letting out a point-blank beam at the dragon's head.

Jim throws tons and tons of ash at the green dragon. Who in turns spews acid to counter. He then forms a ball of ash and tosses at him. Just for it to be countered again by him slashing it in half. His adversary starts laughing at him.

"Why won't you just die!? Who are you anyway?" Jim roared at him frustrated that none of his attacks are connecting.

"I won't die because you are too weak. As for who I am. My name is Rick." The now named Rick said to him. "Remember it for it is the name of your executioner!" He exclaimed before rushing him.

Rick seizes Jim by the wings and smashes him into the ground. "Argh!" Jim could only let before being slammed into a tree. Rick gives up his hold of him. Jim tries to make a swipe at him, only for him to duck out the way. He tries for another attack but stops. Rick is getting ready to fire a stream of acid at him! Forming ash on his wings yet again to block the onslaught.

It is all useless though. The acidic breath burns through the ash. Then the wings are melted off. Earlier than Jim expected the acid hits his face and chest. Jim dies without being able to make a sound. Rick looks over the melted corpse and howls with laughter.

Hydra throws himself into Miles barely staggering him. He starts lashing with his claws. Prior to him being able to do further damage he is slashed. Bloodied puncture wounds from enemy claws. Hydra quickly retaliates with a breath of ice.

This hardly fazes Miles as he just tanks the strike. Flashing his claws, he cuts Hydra across the abdomen. "Aah!" Hydra lets out a gasp of agony. Next Miles balls up his hand and punches him to the floor. He looks condescendingly at Hydra.

"Is that all you can do. If that is the case, then it is time you die." Miles states as he charges up a breath of smoke.

"I will show you what I am capable of!" Hydra exclaimed in fury. Ice slowly covers his body like armor. Ice spikes emerging from the wings, tail, and arms. His wings fully encased in ice, looking like there are sickles coming from the bottom of the wings. Hydra's tail ending with a spear shaped tip with spikes coming from the sides. The arms covered in layers of thick ice. Three ice blades protruded on each arm.

Hydra's head looks to have a frosty crown. Four solid ice horns facing backwards. In addition to the crown, two ice fangs hang from his face. His frosty armor couldn't have formed at a better time. He is protected from a beam of smoke. The armor not having a mark on it.

"Well look at that. Your attack had no effect on me." Hydra said a little bit smug. Staring at his opponent with a smirk on his face.

Miles just growls in anger, appalled by the ice dragon. "Don't get ahead of yourself. This will make no difference." He snaps at him.

Amongst the tall trees laid varieties of fruit. Also amongst the trees are different types of animals that inhabit them. Of course, many are currently eating the fruit that cultivate here. While others are trying to hunt and eat their neighbors. With the remaining just chilling in the trees.

Then suddenly silence filled the treetops with them all fleeing in terror. Each one of them hiding in their burrows or nest. **Swoosh! Swoosh! Swoosh!** Multiple swoosh sounds are heard from above the trees. After a minute goes by the inhabitants come out after confirming the coast is clear. The peaceful calm slowly comes back.

Felix and a group of hikoyasei fly over the forest. The group of them doing their daily patrols. Nothing seeming out of the ordinary. *"Seems like everything is going fine."* Felix thinks to himself. His mind goes back to the conversation he had with Vladimir and Tsu'tey.

"Now Felix. As you are aware of, we hikoyasei are an old race. While not an ancient one, we still go far back. And our ancestor species was one of the top creatures of their time." Vladimir told him.

"Really? I wasn't aware of that." He said in general surprised. "How high up were they?" Felix politely asked them.

Both Vladimir and Tsu'tey turn to each other. Then they looked back at Felix. "They were on par with the prehistoric limpexes, goliaths, and dragons." Tsu'tey told him in a dead serious tone.

"Really they were that powerful!?" He asked in shock. Staring at them both with large eyes.

"Yes, they were." Tsu'tey answered with a grin. "Not only they a larger size but they had abilities to help them." She finished.

"Our ancestors were called the hikomasen. And they were powerful apex predators." Vladimir added. Looking at Felix and seeing surprise and awe in his face.

"So, what differences did they have from us? If you don't mind me asking." He respectfully inquired.

"Not at all. We did bring this up for a reason." Tsu'tey assured him. "Now speaking of differences, you already know they were stronger than us." She continued. "Another difference was they were the same size as the prehistoric apexes."

Felix looked surprised for a second then thought about it. "I guess that makes sense. Being the same size allows for more equal footing." Felix stated.

"Exactly. Anyhow hikomasens' jaws split open like a barb claw's jaw. As a matter of fact, this helped them use an ability that we will mention later." Vladimir jumps back in. "They also had barbed tails and smaller back wings." He concluded his explanation.

"Oh. That does sound like some interesting traits to have. Did the secondary wings help them fly?" Felix asked in minor confusion.

"Yes, it helped support their weight. Are ready to hear to hear about their special weapons?" Tsu'tey inquired wanting to continue.

"Yes ma'am." He confirmed. Once confirming that he was ready she carried on. "Ok so hikomasens could do a lot more than us." She started off. "One major weapon was they could use high concentrated sound." Tsu'tey stated. Felix's eyes slightly widen but wasn't too shocked.

"The potency of the sound was very high. Capable of shattering rocks, breaking bones, and even disabling certain elemental attacks." Tsu'tey informed him.

"Of course, those were on sub elemental creatures. Seeing how no creature could use elementals yet. Though it is confirmed that the sound could displace water and lava." Vladimir added.

"Now the next ability is one you might recognize." Tsu'tey continued the lecture. "Our ancestors were cable of using silk. Not just balls of it but as streams as well." She vocalized.

"They could also use pure acid." Vladimir informed him of the last trait. Felix looked up in realization.

"That is why we have acidic silk." He assumed in his conclusion. Both chiefs nodded their heads confirming his theory.

"That is right. Now for the reason why we brought it up. As you noticed, hikoyasei don't exhibit these traits. As a whole race our kind can't use any of these abilities." Vladimir spoke remorsefully. "Then we have the fact that we are weaker than the goliaths, dragons, and limpexes." He finished in a sad note.

Felix looks at him. "You mentioned as a whole, we can't do what the hikomasen could. Does that mean there are special cases?" He asked them.

"Yes. You are correct. In fact, me and Vladimir can use pure acid and different forms of silk." She told him letting know about the abilities they have.

"The both of you can use acid?" He in appalment. Flickering his eyes back in forth between them. Surprised at the revelation he had just heard.

The pair of them are amused by his expression. With them being very old it is nice to see the current generation be shocked about anything new. Most other races it's the old that get surprised. Vladimir and Tsu'tey nod their heads towards him.

"Yes, we are very proficient with acid. Which brings us back to why we told you about it. We believe you have potential to use the sonic sound and silk manipulation." Tsu'tey brought the conversation back on topic.

"You really believe I could do this?" He said in disbelief.

"Yes. We believe and will be teaching you how." Vladimir told him in earnest. Felix looked up with a determined look. "I will try my best chiefs." He said with conviction.

His mind went back to the training. While he hasn't master either ability. However, he is now capable of using his new abilities to an extent.

Glancing over to the rest of them he asked. "Hey, do any of you see anything?"

A chorus of no's answered him. A gray hikoyasei sees something out of the corner of his eye. "Hey, what is that?" She called out getting everyone's attention. They all turn to the direction she is staring at. "I don't know but we are going to find out." Felix let them know.

The flock turn and head in the direction of interest. *"I hope it is nothing drastic."* He pleaded in his mind.

"These yellow fangs will make a great addition to the dark quill DNA. Won't be long before we defeat them." A human shaped dark quill concludes in his mind.

His quill shaped hair sticking up in the air. Sporting slitted light gray eyes. He was taller than Ness and White spine but shorter than Ren. Quaint skinny, looking almost like a fleshy skeleton. He was standing a little distance away from the yellow fang colony.

His forces were combating the yellow fangs. Killing and consuming those they could. The objective is to breach the colony, consume the queen and turn this into a hive for the dark quills. A perfect plan he has came up with. His apex will proud of him.

His dark quill forces should do. The hunters he brought are two types. That being behemoth types or bear armadillo variants. Some tower over the yellow fangs. Plenty are also the same size.

Yellow fangs fought back their invaders. A soldier was in the process of impaling a behemoth type in the head. Two drones jump onto a bear armadillo dark quill. Fangs tearing through its body. Another soldier shoots spikes at a hunter. Skewering it with multiple spikes.

"I think I should personally get involved. To speed up the process." He muttered to himself. Letting out a sigh he steps forward.

Barely a minute in the warzone and he was accosted. A trio of drones attempt to pounce on him. The meso quickly seizes the arm of one. Twirling around he smacks one aside and blocks the other. Tearing the yellow fang in his grasp in half.

He throws the two halves at the recovering drone. This allows him to focus on the one lunging at him. Catching him by the jaws he pulls his jaw apart. Walking up to the last one plunges his hand through the side.

Chapter 21

Crystal bushes glow in the darkness of the night. All sorts of critters move about across the sand. Each one of them enjoying the night. However, even these animals know better than to trespass on the battlefield. Every one of them knowing that spells death.

A mutilated behemoth dark quill drops to the ground. It's killer in the process of killing another hunter. Right before he could an alpha berserker intercepts him. Claws of the dark quill tear into the goliath bringing him to the sandy ground. Grasping his head and heaving, the alpha removes the goliath's head.

Right before it could find its next target a clawed hand emerges from its torso. Grasping it with her other hand, Dawn rips the alpha apart. Backflipping into the air saves her from the mandibles of another alpha. The alpha turns around and charges her. She waits for it to get close, then at the right moment thrusts her hand out. Her claws impale the alpha and with its momentum proceeds to split it down the middle.

Tossing the body to the right of her, Dawn eyes moved across the battlefield. A pack of hunters were racing towards her. Dawn forms a wooden shield to protect herself. They leaped up and tried to attack her. With her shield protecting her she throws them back.

"There is a lot these things." She thought as see stared at the millions of dark quills. She glances at the hunters she just tossed back. Before they could recover, Dawn ejects large wooden spikes from her left arm. Each one of them connecting to a hunter. Seeing them all skewered, she turns back to the battle.

There running towards her is another alpha. This one being a moth ray looking one. *"All I know is this one will die just like the rest. Let's get this over with."* Dawn moves to combat it.

Von rolls back escaping a large fist that impacted the area he was just in. The alpha's fist craters the ground. The koatl dark quill opens its spits black acid. He shifts to the right to avoid the acid. Then buries his left hand into dirt. In a quick motion throws the dirt into the alpha's face.

Swinging its head back and forth. The dark quill tries to remove the dirt from its face. Using the time, he bought himself gets ready. Covering his hands in acid he jumps forward. Nailing one of its arms as the acid its through it.

Hissing in pain it growls at Von. Before he could follow up his attack, it coils around him. Slowly it starts to constrict him. "This hurts a bit. Nevertheless, you are going to have to try harder." Acid starts being secreted from his body. The acid comes in contact with the dark quill.

Aah! Aah! Argh! Its body starts melting. Withering in pain as it disconnects from Von. Not like it can do much now. With its body falling apart it lets out a wail. Von looks at the deceased creature with a mild smirk.

"Told you it would take more than that." Von chuckles a bit.

Swiveling his head, a bit he sees a small dark quill killing goliaths with ease. Staring at it he could only think, "Well this might be a problem."

Ren dodges a crystal goliath as it tries to stomp him. Hopping up he manages to land on its arm. Running along the arm, he jumps over a swipe made at him.

Reaching its head, he plunges his hands into its skull. Body ceasing all movement the goliath falls to ground. Leaping off the body he turns to look at it. Shrugging his shoulders in a nonchalant manner.

"That was kind of fun." Ren boredly says before heading to another goliath.

Four alpha type dark quills tackle Ivan. With their combined weight brings him to the ground. All in tandem press down on him to keep him down.

Unfortunately for them, metal spikes impale them before they could do anything else. The blood covered spikes emerging from their bodies retract. Tossing the corpses of him Ivan dust of his hands.

"Suckers really thought it was going to be easy." He whispered.

Looking behind himself he sees a group of krypto hunters ganging up on someone. "Well let me help this poor fellow out," He quickly rushes to aid them. Running up to them he starts to help.

Lashing out his claws severs the upper half of one hunter. "Back off you little beasts," Ivan stomps down on another. His foot crushing it beneath.

Many hunters turn to face the new threat. Which allows the now relieved green goliath some breathing room. Thanks to this he can now fight properly.

Together they are both able to finish of the pack of hunters. The green goliath lets out a sigh of relief. "That was close. I was almost a goner," He turns to Ivan, "Thank you for the help. I don't think I would have made it."

"No need for thanks. Us goliaths need to stick together. Especially against whatever these things are." Ivan assured the other goliath.

"Now let's protect our home," Both goliaths rush back into the battle.

Ivan extends a metal blade from his arm and cuts a uropygid alpha in half. Then hits a hybodus hunter with his tail. He spikes killing it.

Helga caves in the dark quill koatl's head with her foot. Grabbing its body, she uses it like a whip. Whipping an alpha away from her. Then she crushes a hunter with her whip.

"That was kind of fun." She said to herself. Rotating her head, she sees more dark quills running towards her.

"Well, that is a good number of them." Staring at the hunters she come to a decision. "Let's even the odds," Helga looks to the ground.

Shoving her hands into the soil, small amounts of sand leave her body. "This should do," Helga watches as the sand mixes with the soil on the ground. The sand starts to take shape and form.

Multiple sand creations form and stand attention. They took the shape of a saurian creature. Glancing at her creations she nods.

"Alright, this is good enough." She turns back to the hunters, who are now only feet away from her. With a mental command sends the constructions at them.

Sand saurians attack the hybodus hunters. Glass teeth bite into dark quill flesh. A hybodus smashes a saurian's head.

Helga looks at the battle. *"Well let's armor up,"* Sand starts forming over her bumpy skin. Harding over her skin. Glass spikes sprouting from her back and shoulders. Blades of glass on the tip of her tail. Large sickles made of glass on her arms. Finally, a crest of glass adores her head.

Opening her mouth, lower jaw splitting open. Tongue hanging out as she flicks it in the air. Closing her mouth, she lets out a smirk. "Well time for an extermination," Rushing to an unexpecting hunter.

Within a second she cuts it in half. Turning on a dime she spots a moth ray alpha. Rushing forward she cuts off its arms then its head.

Felix and the others arrive to where the commotion is. Looking down they all are appalled and infuriated at what they see. Hundreds of dark quills swarm the hive of yellow fangs.

"Is that what I think it is?" One of them said bitterly. Another, nods at their question.

Felix turns to a pair of hikoyasei "Go and warn the chiefs. Everyone needs to know about this."

"Yes sir," Both of them nodding as they fly off. Turning back to stare down the dark quills. Remembering what they did to them. All actions must be punished. They will learn not to invade our territory.

"Alright listen up. I say it is time to pay back these creatures." Felix informed them. "Plus, we can't let them take over our new home."

"Yeah," Multiple shouts of agreement are let out. Hikoyasei glance down at their hated adversary. What happened at the mountains isn't going to happen again.

This time they are ready. They are not the ones being ambushed here. The ambushing will be done by them. No closed spaces to confined them. Now they know what they are dealing with.

"Thinking on it. This going to be what happened with the dragons." Felix thought with mild amusement.

That's right we are going to send them back like the dragons did. Only difference being there will be no survivors. This will be a cleansing. These abominations will be eradicated.

"Now let's eliminate these threats" Moving to the warzone. The rest of the flock follow him. The time of battle is ahead.

"Hope you are ready you scum bags. Time for you pay for all lives you took." He grumbled.

Yellow fangs fail to hit the meso. A soldier shoots her spikes at him. None connect as he dodges out of the way. Shaking his head in exasperation.

"These yellow fangs have more tenacity than I thought." He turns to see the soldier that fired at him. It rushes towards. Hopping to the side he grabs her leg. Then yanks it backward.

Grasping the back of her neck and applying pressure. With a quick squeeze he breaks the creature's neck. Dropping the body onto floor causally. Crunching of leaves snaps him into attention. Twisting around to the noise his back quills swishing in the air.

A drone was thrusting both his tails at him. Catching both its tails in his hands. "Good attempt," He scoffs as he tosses the drone to the ground. As it stumbles to the side, he seizes a middle arm lifts him. "Not good enough though."

Instantly slamming the yellow fang into the ground. Raising his foot and brings it down on its spine. Leaving a bloodied mess in its place. Turning around to see the battle barely changing.

A dark quill attacks a yellow fang. Fangs cutting into its neck. One hunter is felled by a drone. Who removes his tails from the hunter's head. In the background a soldier has her skull crushed in the jaws of a dark quill.

He lets out a sigh. "Maybe I should speed things along. Transforming should help."

"Then again. I don't like shifting," He shakes his head. Examining the hive guards. "Yeah, won't be necessary."

"I did think we would be in the hive by now. We are close to entering." He nods to himself. *"Yeah, just need patience,"* Turning to stare at some hunters.

The group of dark quills are then caught in a clump of silk. It quickly restrains their movements. Without warning they are just fastened to the ground. Not missing a second yellow fang drones attack and kill the incapacitated hunters.

Eyes widening in shock at what he just saw. His hunters were just covered in silk. He didn't know yellow fangs produce silk. Did they? Another glob silk captures some dark quills with soldiers finishing them off.

"What the!? What is happen-," He is interrupted by giant bats slamming into his forces.

"Giant bats? Why are they here?" He questioned not understanding.

"Prepare to die vermin!" Felix roars at the dark quill mass. He turns his head to focus ahead.

The dark quills are now starting to struggle in this conflict. With the combined might of the yellow fangs and hikoyasei they start to falter. Hikoyasei snatch up hunters and bite into them. While yellow fangs attack the wounded, trapped, or distracted ones.

The drones and soldiers seem to avoid the flock of bats. Not running from or to them. Which works out perfectly for them.

"Good the yellow fangs are not attacking any of us." Felix stated. "Guess they don't see us as a threat. Woo, I was worried for a second."

Felix starts looking around. "Where is that wretch leader of theirs is. She must pay for what she has done," He continues to search for her. Out the corner of his eye, he sees the suppose leader.

A hikoyasei crashes into the meso sending him tumbling across the ground. Before he could move, he is grabbed and tossed into the air. With his body gliding through the air, he catches his bearings. Carefully landing he spares at the hikoyasei.

"How dare you! You filthy creatures!" He shouts angrily at the hikoyasei.

One of the large attempts to hit with a silk ball. He hops over the ball. As his feet touches the ground the hikoyasei tries to attack him. Catching one of its claws he slams it into the floor. Breaking its wrist in the process.

As it is brought to the floor, he seizes its jaws. Pulling the jaw and skull in opposite directions. **Aah! Shriek! Argh!** The squeals of pain are heard from the hikoyasei. Mouth blooding as it tears apart.

"Ness was right," He tosses the corpse to the floor. "These hikoyasei are weak."

More oversized bats come to attack him. It becomes a one-sided slaughter in a matter of moments. Clawed hands easily tear through fur and flesh. Swinging a severed arm, he beats a hikoyasei to death. Then he throws it at a flying one knocking it from the air.

"Once I kill all these bats, I can continue with my task." He spoke. Turning to a larger hikoyasei which was coming towards him.

"Huh. Time to kill another one." He tries to snatch it from the air. The hikoyasei spins out of the way.

With a quick turn he catches the meso and starts to crush him. Then throws him into the rocky walls. "Your fight is with me abomination," Felix informs the dark quill leader.

Chapter 22

Not liking the cocky smirk on his face, he rushes to knock it off. Miles swings his left claw at Hydra's shoulder. **Clink!** Unfortunately, his claws bounce off the ice armor. The sound reverberating in the space around them. Hydra smirks deepens as he looks at the older dragon.

"Well look at that," Hydra chuckles and stares at Miles. "Doesn't look like you can break my armor." He finishes with a shrug.

"Don't think this is over. You will die all the same." Miles growls towards.

"Whatever you say smoky." Hydra says with a coy smile.

Having enough of this Miles attempts to blast him smoke. Not wasting a second Hydra dives out of the way. The beam of smoke burns part of the clearing. Many trees falling apart.

Miles then tries to ram into him. Hydra flies above him to dodge him. He then tries to swipe at the smoke dragon. But Miles sees this and maneuvers out of the way.

Hydra struggles to fire a beam of ice towards him. Miles is too slipper to hit, however. He stops releasing the beam and Miles goes on the attack. His tail slams into him but doesn't even scratch the ice.

Miles lets out a tsk seeing his attack fail again. This though allows Hydra an opportunity. Flapping his wings, he positions himself under the larger dragon. Lining himself up he attacks Miles' abdomen with his ice-covered claws.

The smoke dragon lets out pained groan. Gashes spread out around his underbelly. Blood dripping from the wound.

"That hurt huh?" Hydra said.

The stone dragon stares at his fallen foe with distain. Beating his wings, he flies away to support Jim. As he approaches, he catches a glimpse of a large, bloodied puddle. His heart dropped as he recognized that it was Jim.

"No! Not Jim! I lost both of my disciples today." He thought remorseful. *"They both had a bright future ahead. And both were killed by this bastard!"*

Tom was filled with rage at the death of his underlings. Flying to the acid dragon intent on avenging his students. Balling his palm into a fist Tom strikes Rick fist drilling into the side of his head. Rick stumbling back as he tries to reorient himself.

"You will pay for killing Jim and Roy!" Tom roared. Landing little distance away.

"Oh, I am going pay for ending those two children's lives? They were weak and so are you." He laughed.

"You will soon join them," A grin grew on his face. Moving his head out the way of a tail slap. Laughing at the clumsy dragon Rick lashes his claws against Tom's face.

"Aah," Clutching his slightly crack claws. Eye twitching in irritation at this development. Lifting his head to look at his opponent.

"Did you really think your weak claws could pierce my stony scales? That just foolishness." Tom told him.

Without wasting a second he lets out a breath of stone. Rick just has enough room to dodge the blast. Taking the chance, he answers in kind. Coating his hand in acid, he takes a swing at Tom's right shoulder.

"Aah!" Tom groans as he glances at his shoulder. Parts of it were dissolved or dissolving. He turns back at Rick with a glare.

"That should do the trick." Rick said coldly.

Miles slams his claws across Hydra's head. Besides turning his head, it did nothing. Hydra quickly headbutts Miles. This makes him stagger back. Hydra spreads his wings making frost come off.

Thanks to the cold air from the frosty armor, clouds started to form. This works in Hydra's favor. With the clouds blocking the sun there is less heat baring down on him. While the sun's rays wouldn't melt the ice, it does help to have the area colder. Which happens with the clouds chilling the place.

The colder the area the more a cold variant dragon could do. While icy regions would be better for him this is still good scenario for him.

Having the air get colder will allow Hydra an easier time multiplying the environment here. Looking pleased as it all comes together.

Opening his jaws and breathing a ray of ice. The torrent of ice zooming to the black dragon. Miles only has enough time to avoid majority of the blast. He flinches in pain as part of his wing and arm frostbitten.

Before Miles could even catch his bearings, he hollers in pain from a jab. Hydra removes his ice tipped from his thigh. Blood dripping from the puncture wound.

"Did that hurt? Well, my bad about you being weak." Hydra snarked. *"Oh, that really made him mad now."*

Miles stares at him with a look of bloody murder. Without wasting time spews torrents of smoke. Answering in kind blasts him with ice. The ice beam speared through the torrent of smoke and hit its target.

Miles holds back a scream as he is blasted. Hydra fires two more ice breaths at him. One managing to hit him.

"You are not going to escape," He flies towards him. Claws barely grazing him.

"You are the one that needs to escape," Forming a ball of smoke in his hand. Then hurls at the ice dragon. Who counters by forming a barrier of ice.

"I need to go ahead and kill him." Hydra thinks in mind. *"I just need an opportunity."* He finishes his thought.

Feeling around he notices a change in temperature. Its cold enough that the clouds fully formed. This gives Hydra an idea. Chances are this might finally kill the accursed dragon. Hydra turns and stares at the clouds.

Miles starts to form a ball of smoke above his wings. He stops as he notices a shift in temperature right on top of him. Ice sickles and shards begin to form over Miles. Once they finished forming it rained ice. He stabbed by many before he could react.

The ice rain lasted for a couple moments. Miles has fallen to the earth from the barrage. Ice spikes protruding from his body. Hydra stares down at him with a look of satisfaction.

"Finally, he is dead. All roar and no bite." Hydra shook his head in amusement.

A groan of pain catches his attention. He looks down with wide eyes as Miles is still alive. Slowly but surely, Miles got back on his feet. Then painfully he stood up on his back legs.

Moving his head to stare at Hydra who suddenly got a chill. Blood falling from different parts of him he gives Hydra a hatefully death glare.

"Yo-Youu-!" He tried to wheeze out. Shuddering and trying to catch his breath.

Hydra calmed down thinking this is over. He would be proven wrong. The ice start to melt off Miles. "YOU WILL DIE!" He shouts in pure anger.

Before he could move Tom slams his tail across Rick's head. The amount force used makes him tumble over the ground. Luckily for him he still had his wits about him. Leaping away from another tail strike that would have caved in his head.

Rick then charges toward Tom. Grapples him and tries to tackle him. Which is a stupid move, "Do you really think you are going to out muscle me?" Pressing down on him with his superior weight.

With anticipation of being crushed Rick starts secreting acid. Acid starts eating at Tom's paws. "Aah," Recoiling from the painful burns. Rick backs away from the stone dragon.

Rick takes off into the sky. Figuring it is stupid to fight a stone dragon on the ground in a physical match. Tom quickly follows him to the air. Which was probably an ill-advised decision on his part.

Tom attempts to bite the acid dragon's leg. With immense speed Rick maneuvers out of harm's way. Tom quickly swings his tail aiming for his wing. Rick ducks out of the way.

"You may have had me on the ground, but up here you don't stand a chance." Rick taunts Tom.

"It won't make a difference if we are up here or down there. You will die for what you did!" He bellows in fury.

Spewing thousands of stones from his maw. The acid dragon sends globs of acid to counter the beam. Moving to the side of Tom to stay of the way of the rest of the beam.

Forming spikes over his body to help in this endeavor. Proceeding eject the spikes at Rick hoping to impale him. The green dragon releases a stream of acid. Rotating his head to melt all the spikes. Tom then attempts to plunge into him.

Weaving around the larger and bulkier dragon with ease. He goes for another strike, but it is dodged as well. None of the earth dragon species are known for their aerial combat. Not to say that they are terrible fighters in the air. Just not the best.

Now tin and aluminum dragons are light enough to succeed in good aerial combat. However, all earth types are better land fighters. Which is why they prefer to fight on the ground.

Not to say acid dragons are great air fighters. Because they are not known for air combat either. They however are lighter and faster than stone dragons. Which is the crux of the problem.

Tom cannot keep up with Rick's superior speed. And he is going to pay for it. Taking the chance Rick flies above Tom. Forming a ball of acid, he targets his back. Throwing the ball at him, once it's the correct size.

"Aah!" Tom screams as acid eats through his stone armor. He tries to cover himself with more stone. But he is not fast enough. "Got you," Rick lets out a breath of acid on Tom's wings.

"Argh! Aah!" He shouts out in pain. Without the function of his wings, he plummets to the earth. Crashing into the ground leaving a crater. As he tries to get up acid splashes into his front legs.

"Aah!" He squeals. Rick lands next to him with a grin. Walking up to him he stares down at him. Shaking his head in amusement.

"Looks to me that you will not be avenging those weaklings. How sad." He said mockingly. Grabbing Tom by the neck with his jaws he bites through his neck. Nearly decapitating it.

Hydra could only fill dread from the sound of Miles voice. The ice fully evaporated from his body. Even the blood was steaming. He looked he was ready to go again.

There has always been distinction between elements. Just like how some are better flyers there is a gap between temperature types. All cold type dragons whether it was ice, frost, mist, or fog are weak against heat types. Even though the cold dragons have the ability to make more types of attacks. There is reason they fight heat types in pre-cold areas.

Hydra was about to be reminded of that fact. Cold dragons always try to kill heat dragons quickly. He should have finished off Miles when had the chance.

"I am going to enjoy burning you to ash!" He snarled as blood covered his face.

The temperature started rising. The blood started boiling off Miles. Clouds started to disperse from the heat. Now with gone the sun shines back down on them. With the light Hydra could get a better look at the smoke dragon.

What he saw unnerved him. Loads of wounds littered his body with some on his head. Thanks to the heat the wounds were sealed tight. Smoke started to emit from Miles.

"I won't let do anything." Hydra said as breaths a torrent of ice.

The icy beam heads towards Miles. Miles just creates a shield of smoke to block the attack. More smoke comes off him as it starts to fill the area. Launching himself forward Hydra tries to punch him. All Miles does is form a smoke tornado.

"Woah!" He lets out as he is dragged by the tornado. With a sudden burst of ice, he disperses the tornado. Spinning himself to face Miles all he sees is smoke. The whole area is filled with smoke.

"Come out coward! You won't escape!" Hydra yelled in annoyance. Irritated that Miles can't be seen.

He wouldn't have to wait long. Miles emerges from the smoke on his right. Smoke covered claws scratch the ice armor. Hydra notices that there is a crack on now. Before Miles can attack again Hydra throws a sphere of ice at him. Causing him to retreat into the smoke.

With all the smoke around him Hydra's armor is slowly weakening. He stares all around him trying to find the black dragon. Not waiting for an attack starts firing an ice beam. Moving the beam across in a circle motion to hit as much as possible.

Ice cuts through everything in path. Yet there is still nothing. Then he sees Miles emerging. Or what he thought was Miles as multiple smoke dragons emerge. The dragons surrounding him.

"Well, this might be troublesome." He said in a deadpanned tone.

They all begin to rush him. Curling his wings and spinning he fires spikes from his body. Each one of the smoke dragons are hit. They all explode into smoke. Extra smoke clones come to attack him.

"At least it won't be hard getting rid of them." He said to himself.

A clone's claw strikes his shoulder. Breaking the armor further. Spinning in place cutting all of them with his sharp tail. Smoke leaving all their forms.

With the smoke distracting him he couldn't see Miles coming in. Claws carve into his wings. Miles' claws just hot enough to slash through the armor. Fortunately for Hydra his flesh is just grazed.

Hydra whirls around and tries to blast him. He darts out of the way. Then he releases a beam of his own. His smoke targeting Hydra's wings. The frosty armor shattered around his wings and back. Smoke burning his flesh as his wings are destroyed.

"Got you! You little pest!" Miles glared at the falling Hydra. "Let's see you escape this!" Opening his mouth to release another blast.

The ray of smoke smashes into his chest and arms. Hydra lets out another scream of pain. Pain all around his chest, forelegs, back, and what is left of his wings. *"Is this how it ends,"* He thought as he crashes back into the ground of naviros.

Hydra attempts to lift himself up. Before he could find any purchase Miles impacted his back. "You won't be getting up," His nails digging into his flesh. Miles then grasps Hydra's head and lifts it up. Hydra tries to struggle out of hold. Seizing his jaws, he starts to pry it open. Once his mouth was wide enough, he started spewing smoke down his throat. Hydra thrashed all about in pain. His struggles however start to fade. All color in his body leaves his body.

"Finally, he is dead. Such an annoyance." Miles huffed out.

Looking around he perceives that his smoke wall is still up. *"Let me bring this down to see how my partners fared."* He removes the smoke from the area.

Once the smoke recedes, he sees Rick in distance. Who seems to have some wounds. Flying over to him to see if he won already. Reaching him he sees both the stone and ash dragon corpses. He lands next to him.

"I see you are doing well." Miles commented.

"Yeah, the fight wasn't that hard." Rick huffed back.

"I see you killed the remaining two." He looks to the green dragon. "What lead to that?"

"Sparky got killed by stony over here." Rick shakes his head in disappointment.

"Well, that is a shame." Miles shrugged his shoulders.

"Are you sad that I got two more kills than you?" Rick asked with a smirk.

"Nonsense. Besides we both know who is the strongest out of the both of us." He said back.

Right before they could continue talking, a beam of obsidian engulfs Rick's head. His headless carcass hit the floor. Miles is shocked but snaps out of it in time to escape a blast of fog. He starts to fly away but his legs are hit with a breath of venom.

"Aah!" He screams as his legs corrode away. Miles continues to fly away in pain. Calamity looks down at their fallen allies. "Viper, Mist stay here and see if there is a chance Hydra survived." He commanded.

"Yes sir." Both said to him. He goes to chase after Miles. The two of them land next to Hydra's body. Mist starts to examine his body.

Chapter 23

Marie propels herself with a jet of acid over a group of hunters. Staring down at them contemplates how things ended up like this. *"Seriously what are these things."* Gravity takes hold of her as she plummets back down. Using her time, she forms a ball of acid.

Right before she lands, she drops the acid ball on top of them. They could only scream as the acid ate through their flesh and bones. She landed on their melted bodies. Maria turns to look around the battlefield.

"Dang. This won't be ending anytime soon." She concluded.

The battle seemed even for now. Both sides were facing loses to each other. On one side we see goliaths winning and gaining ground. While the other side the dark quills are advancing kill all in their way. All-out war was happening.

One goliath slams an alpha to the ground. Finishing it off with a stomp to the head. Another goliath is taken by surprise by an alpha. Jumping on his back and biting the back of his head. It wasn't long before it killed him.

"Well at least we are making a dent in them." Maria mumbles.

Snapping at attention as more hunters charge at her. Firing torrents of acid decimate their charge. However, many reach her and clawing her. Maria stomps and bites many of them. Cutting many in half with her claws.

She fights off many with ease. Unfortunately, many come to assault her. Maria is swarmed by dozens of hybodus dark quills. No matter how much she fought. Or acid she used to melt them. There too many for her to kill. With their numbers they overcame her. Teeth sinking in and tearing her apart.

Soo-Yun's claws impale a berserker alpha in its head. Pulling back, she throws the body to a trio of hunters crushing them under it. Flicking the

154

blue blood of her nails. She rushes to grab a hunter in her hands. With a little effort rips him in half.

Soo-Yun couldn't even smile right now. Her bubbly attitude switched for her blood thirsty one. Snatching a leaping koatl by its head. She pops it like a grape. Blue liquid splashing her.

"I hope the others are fine," Smacking away a hunter with her tail. Turning to face moth ray dark quill. Soo-Yun leans her head back as the alpha tries to bite off her face. Twisting on her heels she kicks it away. Spitting a glob of plasma at it.

"That was a little close for comfort." She pondered.

A group of dark quill behemoths run her way. Claws covered and glowing with she slashes apart the dark quills one by one. Catching one that tried to jump on her. She quickly burns it to death. Tossing its remains.

Turning her head, she was able to discern the corpse of a familiar person. "No not Maria," She starts to feel the bloodlust rise in her. Facing a group of alphas coming to challenge her. Her body starts glowing with plasma energy.

Staring at her enemies Soo-Yun forms plasma in her mouth. Planning to vaporize the bastards. Concentrating on the plasma in her in her mouth she lets out a thin beam. Cutting its way through all of them like they were made of water.

Huffing as she looks back at her dead friend. "I will avenge you, Maria. I will exterminate them all." She mutters before running on all fours to kill more dark quills.

He doesn't understand how it came to this. The white and black creatures were more than some type of disease. All around he witnesses the slaughter of his comrades. Only thing holding together him is the fact they are making a dent in the enemy forces.

"I hope my group is ok." He wished with his heart.

The leaf goliath has seen better days. To be honest he could fall at any moment. However, he fights on to stop the invaders. No matter the numbers of wounds on him.

Calmar tears off a hunter from his shoulder. Blood dripping from his shoulder. Bloodied wounds covering his body. He was not having good time. Crushing the dark quill in his hand. Tossing at another hunter making it tumble.

Which allows him to step on it levigating it under his weight. Leaving a bloody smear on the ground. Grabbing a krypto hunter in jaws. His teeth making short work of it.

The remains dropping from his mouth. Calmar snarled with his blue stained teeth. Pivoted to the sound of movement by him. Although of him hearing it he wasn't quick enough. An uropygid dark quill tackles him to the ground.

"Argh!" He lets out as mandibles bite into his shoulder. Sooner than he could move the mandibles seized Calmar's throat. Fangs piercing with ease. The life starts to fade from his eyes.

"Please everyone, survive and win these." Was his final contemplation.

Calmar's body slumps to the floor. Life fulling leaving it. Nothing more than a husk.

She smashes an alpha's head with her hand. The beast's head no longer recognizable. Spinning around she stabs a hunter with her tail. Smashing it to the ground. Claire then tackles a berserker dark quill to the ground.

"You guys are relentless," She extends her claws. Then her claws started spinning like a drill. Plunging it into the dark quill's chest. Pulling up Claire splits its upper torso in half.

"Another dead. Well, more to kill." She huffed. *"How many more are there?"*

Her thoughts were interrupted by more hunters. Prior to this they had surrounded her. Now dozens race to attack her. Claire couldn't prevent from piling on top of her. All going for the kill.

Woefully for them that would not be the case. Spikes are quickly inserted into their bodies. Erupting from their backs violently. Many dead dark quills hang from metallic spikes. Retracting her spikes, the corpses hit the floor of the desert.

Standing at full height Claire looks around. She tsk as more dark quills coming charging in. Morphing her right arm into the shape of a gun she unloads onto the coming forces. She grins.

The shots decimate her adversaries. She rotates her head to see how everyone else is faring. Some are dying left and right. Others are victorious in their battles.

"That's good. I don't think-." She stops her thought as she notices something.

Many of her fellow goliaths are being killed off without mercy. All by a small dark quill. The one leading this attack. That one among them all, needs to die Claire thought. She runs to the location that she sees him at.

Ren removes his hand from a purple goliath's knee. Which forces it to the floor. Giving him the opportunity to sprint towards its face. Pining its head down with one hand. He raises the other and plunges into the skull of the beast.

Flicking the animal's blood of his claws. Movement catches his attention. Rolling under a blast from another goliath. Righting himself he moves to kill it. Extending his claws, Ren cuts into the leg of the goliath. Then rolls under another.

"They never learn," Climbing the orange goliath. Right as it tries to grab him, he impales it with his claws. It lets out scream, which is silenced when he decapitates it. "That's another down," he says as he jumps off.

Once he lands, he swiftly runs towards the green goliath. It still struggling to get up from nearly losing its leg. Leaping up Ren grasps its head. Getting a hold of its jaws he pulls its head apart.

"This is really-fun. I glad we are decimating their numbers. Their DNA will be a great addition to our forces." Ren said with a smirk.

"I will make sure to eat one of the stronger ones." He mumbled.

Suddenly he froze up. A metal spike erupts from his chest. Looking down he stares at it. "Got you." He points his head up and sees a metallic goliath.

"Time to end this." Claire growled.

Ren just stared at her and laughed. "You are truly amusing. Though great job getting a hit in." She throws him into the air ready to kill him.

Lily launches globs of slime at her attackers. The krypto hunters are caught in the slime barrage. Withering in the slime as they slowly dissolve. Tossing ball of slime at a hunter engulfing its head in as it blows up.

"Do you, things ever stop coming?!" She asked irritated.

Her answer is 2 alphas rushing towards her. Huffing Lily hops over them. Spinning in the air as she does so. Shifting slime over her hand in the shape of a lance. She then hardens it. Landing behind the pair, Lily turns with speed and stabs one through the back.

Filling the dark quill with slime from the lance. It releases a squeal as the slime eats through body. Just as fast as she does this, she cuts off the other one's head.

"Well at least they are not that hard. These is already a nightmare as it is." Lily sighed.

Glancing to the side of her she sees Claire fighting the dark quill meso. Well, it wasn't really a fight. The meso was leading her around the whole fight. He was dodging all her attacks. But she couldn't dodge his. He cuts her across her chest.

"Ooh. Claire might need some help." Lily thought.

Just as she finished this thought Ren got hold of one Claire's arms. With no effort pulls her arm off. Twirling it around smacks her with it. Lily eyes widens as she sees this.

"Claire I am coming! Just hang on!" She shouted with all her heart.

Lily started sprinting to her mentor. Hoping to save her life. Many hunters stepped in her way. She didn't let them stop her. Smacking them out of the way with her claws.

Nothing was going to stop her from protecting her teacher. She was going to kill this thing.

He weaves out of the way of a moth ray alpha tail strike. Grabbing the tail Leon starts to swing the dark quill around. Then he smashes it into the ground dazing it. Before it can recover, he jumps on it.

He penetrates its head with his claws. Retching its head apart. Brain and blood contents spilling from it. Dropping the body with disregard. Looking to his next opponent.

Leon cuts a koatl alpha in half. Spinning on his heel he stabs a dark quill uropygid in the head. Snatching his claws from it making the cadaver fall. Flicking the fluids from his hands.

Glancing around he looks to spot his next enemy. Eyes widening as he watches Lily being manhandled. He runs to assist her. Seizing a random hybodus hunter and tearing it in two.

"Hope I can help her in time." Leon thought worriedly.

Reaching her he slams his tail into Ren. Sending him flying. Ren rights himself and settles onto his feet. Leon helps Lily up from the ground. Lily nods to him.

"You, ok?" He asked her.

"Yeah. I am but Claire isn't." She said with some despair.

Leon turns to see the unmoving form of the metallic goliath. Arm torn out of its socket. Legs mangled and unable to function. And finally, her head was beaten close to that of a melon.

"Dang. Well let's avenge her then." He says determinedly.

"Yeah. Let's avenge her." She said back.

Both turn to the meso who just watches them. He holds out his and beckoned them to him. Both run to him ready to end his life. He is happy to end their lives.

River's jaws clamp down on a koatl dark quill. Jaws blood stained. Swinging his hands, he intercepts another dark quill charging him. Head held in his hands. With a quick twist River snaps the dark quill's neck.

"This getting us nowhere." He shook his head.

Firing a spike into a hunter killing it. He is then rammed by an uropygid alpha. Nearly barreling over. River however manages to stand on his feet. It goes for another charge.

Outstretching his hand, he catches it by the head. Putting a stop to its charge. He moves his head to the right to avoid its bladed tail. River slowly starts to apply pressure on its head. The alpha squeals, as its head is crushed like a watermelon.

"Well, there goes that one." He neutrally thought.

A swooshing sound is the only warning River is given. Ducking under a berserker's swing. Taking his chance, he goes to disembowel it. The alpha isn't fast enough to escape the attack. River's claws stab right through the beast.

Dragging down his claws he retches open its abdomen. All its innards come spilling out. Every bit of it hitting the desert sand. The corpse falls on top of the disgusting pile.

River is then slammed into. Before he could get his bearings a koatl and moth ray grips his arms. Both with all their might rip off his arms. River lets out a pained scream. The moth ray alpha moves its head to his face.

Spreading open its mouth to show the barbed tongue. In an instant it fires its tongue into his head. Reeling back in it leave a massive hole in River's head. The dark quills waste no time feasting on his body.

Explosions after explosions ran through the collections of dark quills. It didn't matter where they walked or ran to. They were met with explosions. Dark quill limbs were be blasted into the air. Making it rain body parts.

And at the center was her. Throwing whatever bits, she felt like to blow them. Laughing all the way. Picking up a rock and covering it powder she hurls to a group of hunters. **Boom! Boom!**

"This is fun." She couldn't help but think to herself.

Ilya just skipping all about the battlefield. Grabbing a behemoth by the head. She covers it in slime before throwing it to its comrades. **Boom!** Each one dying in the blast.

"This isn't getting old at all." She mutters sarcastically. "Well at least I will have fun with my explosions."

A group of alphas try to pounce on her. She jumps above and releases an explosion on them. Decimating them and breaking the ground. Picking loose bits of rock and dirt she morphs her arm into a gun.

With a smirk on her face, she turns to a couple dark quill hunters. Ilya proceeds to start firing on them. Which causes explosion after explosion. Switching targets, she starts blasting some alphas.

"That's right! Die in the explosions and don't come back!" Ilya howled to the wind.

Rushing forward she punches a charging koatl. Grabbing it she uses like an explosive whip. Whipping it around and blowing away her enemies.

"I wonder what Oliver is up too." She pondered.

An alpha hangs a few inches from the ground. Staring at the corpse with distain, he shakes his head. Oliver removes his blood covered hand from its body. Shaking the blood off as he turns to fight of another alpha.

"This is getting old really quick." He grumbles.

Intercepting mandibles aiming at his shoulder. Oliver pries the mandibles from the beast's head. Backing up the creature screeches in pain. Blood spilling from its mouth. Oliver flips the mandibles in his hands and plunges them into the beast's skull. Letting go of them as it falls.

"Man, we have been fighting for hours. It will be sunrise in a few hours." He shook his head. *"How long are they going to keep coming?"*

Before Oliver could think more about the topic. He is coiled around by a koatl alpha. Biting his shoulder, it starts stabbing him with its legs. "Aah," he lets out as he struggles. The beast starts to constrict him.

Feeling his bones start to strain he knew he had to get out of this. Seeing a chance Oliver sinks his teeth into the spot near its neck. Squawking in agony it releases him. He attempts to plunge his hand into its head. Yet the creature saw it coming jerks out of the way.

Raising up it hisses at him. Staring him down, it spits a glob of acid towards him. Oliver counters by expectorating a black orb. Both attacks smash into each other. This cancels out the attacks.

"You are feisty one." Oliver says with a little smirk.

"Nonetheless, you will die all the same." He stated.

It lets out a roar and charges towards him. The black goliath jumps over the dark quill. It bites into the ground, missing its target. He lands onto the beast. Taking this moment, he starts scratching his opponent.

Ren jumps over a strike from Leon. This leaves him open for an attack from Lily. Lily strikes out of the air. Righting himself before he could hit the ground. Nails digging in the soil to slow him down.

"You both are entertaining. I haven't been having fun until now." He smirked at them.

"You won't be having fun for long." Lily angerly said.

"We are going to wipe that smirk off your face." Leon added.

"Well by all means, try." Ren replied his arms outstretched.

This response angered them both. Running to him to kill him. Leon tries to slam a balled fist on him. Ren moves to left of the fist. Jumping up he kicked Leon in his chin. Making him stumble back.

Not letting him capitalize on the situation. Lily smacks him away from Leon. Leon rights himself and nods to Lily. She forms a ball of slime. Aiming for the recovered Ren she hurls the ball.

Looking at the ball he is hit. It didn't even make him flinch. "What was that supposed to do," He asked. After asking that it explodes. He is flung into the air.

His arm and leg missing. Crashing back into the ground. "That asshole." She said cheekily. Ren regenerates his leg and arm. Standing back up he stares at them.

"Have to admit that was interesting." He calmly stated. Stretching out his newly formed arm.

"What he can regenerate!" Leon shouted.

"Well, we just have to do more damage than he can recover from." Lily stated.

Sprinting forward she attempts to impale him on her claws. Ren ducks under the strike. Faster than she can recover he grabs her hand. Lifting her up he smashes her into sand. Then throws her at Leon who hops over her.

He tries to sink his teeth into Ren. All Ren does is kicks his head away. Causing him to crash into the ground. *"How can he be this strong."* Ren sinks his nails into Leon's thigh. Which causes him groan anguish.

"Let's take a peek at what your spine looks like." Ren says. Laughing as he starts climbing his back.

He doesn't get the chance as Lily hits him with her morphed hand. Her left covered in slime in the shape of a mace. Not letting him recover she slashes him across his chest. Then spits a glob of slime on him. Which hardens keeping him in place.

His chest has already healed from the strike. Forming slime on her other arm and shaping it into a cleaver. She releases a flurry of strikes upon him. Removing his arms and jaws. Leaving lacerates all over him.

Lily stops as she takes an intake of air. Ren quickly recovers from the assault. Cutting off his feet, he jumps at her. Seizing her face as he knees her in the face. She backs up next to Leon who just stands back.

"Damn it! That wasn't enough." Lily yelled frustrated.

"Don't worry. We will get him." Leon comforted her.

Large thorns start to emerge from his body. Blade like thorns adorning his arms. Leon's tail covered in them. And of course, many on his back. Finishing the look hornlike thorns cover his head.

"Well, I guess it is time to take this seriously." Ren said with a shrug. His fangs growing larger with the rest of him.

Chapter 24

"I will be fighting you?" He asked then scoffed. "With how weak your kind is this will be over in a second."

"Such arrogance! Us hikoyasei are not weak!" I stated in my mind. A fire blazing inside with fury. *"I will show you how strong we are!"*

"It won't be that easy." I stared down at the vermin. He just shakes his head in dismissal. He rushes me with immense speed. But I was faster. Flapping my wings, I float above him. Shaking his head in confusion at my escape. Narrowing his eyes at me he tsked. Hopping up he tries to reach me. Couldn't have that now. Twirling out of the way. The meso missed him.

He flips himself and lands on his feet. I move to attack. Releasing a clump of silk to trap him. He looks up only be hit with silk. He grits his teeth as the silk starts burning him. I rush towards him.

"Let's see if your all high and mighty when cut off your limbs." I calmly said.

Slicing through both his arms with my claws. One of his legs quickly following. Before could I start taking away his other, he jumps up. Watching as he grew back his arms. His leg coming back faster than expected.

Shaking his arms to speed up the recovery. The meso just gives me a bored stare. *"Am I boring you! I will show you, bastard!"* I couldn't believe this pest. Looking on like this was some tiresome game.

I only need one good strike to kill him off for good. He regeneration won't help him. I just need to wait for the perfect moment. I fire off some acid silk. This causes him to jump up. Just like I wanted. I quickly fly to him.

Grasping the dark quill commander in my talons, I fly further up. The sensations of him struggling in my feet reach me. It is futile. My grip is too strong for him to escape. I chuckle at his efforts.

"Ok crushing him should work." I concluded. *"And if not then I will rip his broken body to shreds."* My back up plan formed.

I slowly start applying pressure onto the beast. The sound of snapping bones started reach my ears. He starts screaming and tries to escape my clutches. I add more pressure to crush him further. The noise off breaking bones grows louder.

"This will teach him." I thought with a smirk on my face. Lowing my gaze to stare at him. *"Time to end-."* I let out a pained screech.

Staring in disbelief as multiple spikes protrude from my foot. "Aah!" More spikes drill into my foot. Not being able to handle the pain I open my talons. Letting the dark quill leader along with the extended spikes fall to the ground.

Not passing up this chance of invulnerability I proceed on. Raining acid silk over the abomination. Burns show up on his skin. However, his wounds slowly close and heal. He lands on all fours and stands up.

"I will just crush you on the ground." I mumbled.

Skydiving, I slowly approach him. Pivoting my body, I try to squish him under my talons. He hops away, causing me to crater the ground instead. Crawling on all fours I stare him down. He calmly stares back.

Are stare off last for only a minute. I lounged to him planning to crush him in my jaws. He moves to the right of my strike. Causing my head to go pass him. My head is quickly forced back from a kick.

"Ok. That hurt." Shaking the dizziness away. "Time to retaliate." Lashing a claw towards him.

With Felix keeping the dark quill busy the hikoyasei and yellow fangs have had no problems. Both sides have been decimating the hunter forces. If things keep going as it is, it won't be long before they all die.

All over the area there is carnage. Bodies of dark quills strolled about. Corpses ripped apart. Cadavers with spikes sticking out of them. Puddles of blue blood in different spots.

A hikoyasei snatches a dark quill and crushes in its hands. Another stomps a hunter into the ground. Only leaving a blood smear on the grass floor. One hunter is held by the throat from the jaws of a soldier yellow fang. Biting through the neck and decapitated it. Running off to kill some more. Two yellow fang drones have a dark quill in their grasp. Both then begin to rip its arms off. Dropping the arms from their hands. The drones grab a part of it and pull. The dark quill's body stretches as it is torn apart.

Cyan guts spill to the floor covered in blood. Many balls of silk are fire throughout the zone. With a couple striking down hunters. One tries to escape its imprisonment. Only for a soldier to slice through its neck with her claws.

Soaring through a hikoyasei captures a dark quill in its jaws. Grinding it up in its mouth. A giant bat drops a hand full of them from the sky. Causing them to break their bones. Leaving them helpless against the drones and soldiers.

On top of the cliff yellow fang soldiers are sniping. Aiming their tails at the enemy. Spike projectiles firing from the tail tips. Escalating across the field. Drilling into the heads of dark quills.

All around it looks like they are being beat. There isn't much they can do. They are losing ground left and right. They can only hold for so long. Soon their will be none left.

"You are persistent. I will give you that." Dark quill meso spoke. "Nevertheless, you will die. I think I will eat you and gain your power."

"Thanks for the complaint. You are as hard to kill as a stone roach." Felix said back. "But just like them death will be your fate."

Meso just laughed at him. Dashing forward meso approaches Felix. Raising his hand, he attempts to slice into his arm. Lifting his arm out of the way, he prevents that. Then brings down on top of the dark quill.

Instead of pancaking him, meso catches the hand. Pushing up he lifts the hand. The dark quill boss clutches Felix's palm. Tightening his hold, he pulls Felix to the ground then he starts swinging him around.

Gaining enough momentum, he releases him. Sending him flying into a few trees. Getting up from the throw Felix stares at the meso. Grabbing a tree, he throws it at the dark quill. Causing him to back flip from it.

Standing up on his hind legs, he winces a little from the wound from his foot. Felix stands straight up. While not the most comfortable stance for a hikoyasei. They are capable of walking and fighting on their two legs. This well all him to put more force in his hands.

"Ok. Let's see if I can take him out." He pondered to himself.

Tirico K. Bell

He starts running to the meso. Cocking his right arm back. Balling his hand into a fist. Once he reaches him, he punches him. Fist crashing into the dark quill leader.

The meso is nocked to the ground. He swiftly regains his senses. Just in time to dodge an incoming fist. Felix slams down a hand attempting crush the beast. Who propels himself into the air.

Seizing this chance, the hikoyasei catches him with is jaws. He tries to grind him into paste. But only manages to bite off his legs. Legs rapidly growing back. Taking this time to check on the condition of his forces.

Looking around he sees the state of things. It shocks him how bad things have turned out. Staring as group yellow fangs murder some dark quills. The meso gazes at his declining forces. Anger fills him.

Appalled that this seems to be the outcome. They would have won by now if not for the hikoyasei butting in. It's their fault that they are losing. And it is only thanks to their ambush.

"How can this be?! This fight should have been ours." Meso eyes narrowed in fury.

"This isn't the glory that Apex White-spine deserves." He thought grinding his teeth. *"It is these pest's fault that I am failing White-spine."*

His head snapping in Felix's direction. All but snarling at him.

"I have enough of you," He snarls. "Your games will now come to an end. Then I will kill the yellow fangs and take over this region."

His body starts to shift. Sharp quills like a porcupines emerge from his body. Torse expanding to the width of an elephant. Arms bulking up as spikes and quills cover them. Teeth lengthening and sharpening. Head taking a triangular shape. Finally, a tail forms with quills covering it.

The meso is now the size of a whale. Curled tusks adore his face. Spike covered hands with claws as-long as swords. He was sporting a short quill enveloped tail. With his whole body surrounded by spikes and quills.

Clenching his hand. "Now it is time for you to die!" Lunging forward with tremendous speed.

Reaching Felix in an instant. Claws slashes him across his chest. The hikoyasei stumbles back in pain. Five gashes now covering his chest. He briefly covered them with his hands.

Removing his hand, he gets ready for the battle. Meso swings at his head. Ducking under the swing, he goes on the offensive. Outstretching his claws as he brandishes it towards the dark quill. Cutting across its face.

Even as the jaw was falling off. A new one was growing. The abomination goes for another attack. Felix backs up letting its claws pass in front off him. Then he weaves out of the of another.

"He has gotten faster in this form." He couldn't help but think. *"I have to watch out for that."*

Felix strives to land a hit on the boss. All he does is miss, as the beast dodges all the attacks. Moving out of the strike zones last minute. Felix then tries to kick the dark quill. Which is a mistake that will cost him.

The meso evades the kick by dropping down. Seeing how the hikoyasei general is off balance, he strikes. He goes for an upward slash. Felix can't react in time. Meso slices into one of his shoulders. Leaving lined marks behind. "Aah," He stumbles back.

Felix recenters himself. Almost immediately, needs to move his head out of the way. Moving it to the left. The dark quill boss's claws move into the spot his head was. Felix kicks him away.

"That was close." He thought blood pumping. *"A second sooner and I be dead."*

"He is slowing down. Ha. Ha. Predictable." Meso shakes his head. *"Its only matter of time."*

Speedily running to Felix, he reels his arm back. Then launches it forward. Knuckles digging into his gut. Encasing his other arm in spikes, he slams into Felix. Spikes cutting into his flesh, he forced back. A right hook sends him stumbling back.

"Dang it he is too fast." Thoughts flying in his mind. *"The spikes are no joke either."*

Looking back his opponent with his arm encased in spikes. *"Need to fight in the air. I am not fast enough down here."* Felix concluded.

Before he could be attacked again, he flies up into the air. Getting out of range of the dark quill. He starts raining acidic silk over the creature. Firing off so much silk that they casted a large shadow. Clops of silk hit the ground of the area.

Weaving around each glob that would hit him. Even with his large size he was able to dodge each one. Not once getting hit. Thanks to his immense speed dodging wasn't hard.

"Damn it! That didn't work." Glancing around at the strike zone off. *"I have to switch it up a bit."*

Opening his mouth, he fires a stream of silk. Moving in a faster concentrated way than the silk balls. The meso was hit dead on. Silk fastens him to the ground. Covered head to toe in silk.

"That should hold him. Long enough for me to kill him." Felix mumbled.

Contrary to what he thought it didn't hold for long. Sharp quills stab through the white material. Shredding it with ease. Ripping his way out of his cocoon prison. He looks at Felix in an irritated manor.

"Hurry up and die!" He shrieked.

After saying that he grabs a few quills from his back. And with procession throws them near Felix. Fortunately, he was able to get out of the way.

"Ok that failed. I am going to have to try the other thing I learned." Felix figured in his mind.

More quills are thrown rapidly close to him. Spinning all around to avoid them is all he can do. One manages to graze him drawing a little blood. He releases another stream of silk. Capturing his arms.

This temporally stops the spike barrage. Giving himself some breathing room. Allowing himself time to think.

"Ok, let's see how my sonic waves fair." Felix stated in his head.

The meso rips his arms from his confinements. Looking up at the beast that is fighting him. Right as he is about to grab more quills he is stopped. His body is slammed into the ground. The spot cratering.

"Well, it was able to slam him down. Let's see if it will hurt him." Felix spoke.

Opening his mouth, he releases another sonic blast. It connects to the dark quill leader. He coughs up blood as his internal organs rupture. A following blast slams into him breaking his bones. His body stuck in the crater formed.

Felix fires off a couple more sonic beams. Discerning that he won't be getting back up. Flying down next to him to give the death dealing

168

blow. Turning to his hand he covers it with acidic silk. Moving closer he sees the meso.

Watching as it slowly recovers. Blasting it with a few more waves to stop it. Raising his arm Felix smashes down onto his head. Caving in the beast's skull. The acid from the silk eating away at what remains.

"This is what you deserve pest." Venom dripping in Felix's voice.

Looking at the now dead meso he rips it apart. Looking around he spots that all the dark quills are dead. Yellow fangs dragging the corpses to their hive. Leaving the hikoyasei alone. This battle was won.

Chapter 25

Ren stares them both down as he begins the transformation. They both watched him with wide eyes. Feeling astounded as his frame got bigger. Neither one of them were aware that he could do this.

"What in the…?" Leon let out.

"He wasn't even trying?" Lily says in despair. "Was he just toying with us?"

"Yes. I was toying with you both." Said the now finished transformed Ren. "However, you both shouldn't be that upset. You both were more challenging than your fellow kin." He finishes.

Slightly towering the two of them. Standing on 3 toed feet he glances at them. A bulking frame with muscular arms. Sharp clawed hands. Massive spikes sprouting from his back. Having four bladed tentacles hanging from his back. Black patterns covering his tentacles. His head possessing 4 mandibles. Dark gray markings spread out his pale white body.

"But it is time to end this farce." He speaks.

Sending a tentacle towards them. Grabbing Leon by the waist he lifts him up. "Woah," Leon is slammed into the ground. Moving his tentacle Ren smacks him into the dirt again. Slime forms a blade over Lily's am. Before he could further attack Leon, Lily severs the tentacle in half with her slime blade.

"I gotcha," she says as she tries to help him up. Only to get hit by another tendril. Leon is also grabbed by another and thrown. The wounded appendage regenerates. Leon and Lily straighten themselves up. Ren run towards the two of them.

Snatching them both up in tendrils. But that doesn't hold them for long. Leon cuts off the offending tentacle with his thorn blades. Lily has acidic slime roll off her and melt the appendage holding her. Both get ready to attack further, only for Ren to punch them both.

Forcing them to stumble back. Slamming a tendril into Lily's leg, tripping her. Before she could fall, Ren smashes his shoulder into her. Leon jumps onto his back. Biting the deadly limbs.

"Die beast!" He shouts. Tearing off a tenacle with his jaws. Spitting it out. A bladed tip collides with his shoulder. Only to be quickly severed. Ren grasps Leon's head with his hand. Snatching him from his back, Ren throws him into a recovery Lily.

"It will be you vermin who will die." Ren chuckles as his spikes click against each other.

With haste he grabs Lily's arm with his mandibles. "Ah! Let me go," she screeches swiping his face. Lifting her into the air then smashing her into the ground. Raising her he spins her around then throws her away. Leon runs into Ren blades plunging into him.

Lashing his claws slicing through Leon's defenses. Following up with an uppercut to the chin that forces him back. Ren opens his mouth and fires out of bluish ball of energy. The energy crashes into his shoulder burning it. "Ah!" Holding his shoulder.

"Back off of him!" Lily comes back. A slime hammer in hand.

Catching the hammer strike with one of his tentacles. He yanks her towards him. Clubbing her with 3 tendrils. Then kicking to the ground. Spinning around and seizing an incoming punch from Leon.

Tentacles wrapping around his throat as he is lifted. Ren then slams him into Lily. Grabbing her and throwing her in quick procession.

Emil melts the face off an alpha. Crushing its skull as she does so. Releasing the body as it slumps to the floor. Glances at the corpse with no emotion. Shaking her head in exhaustion. She looks around as the battle continues.

"When will this be over." She mumbles.

Since the dark quills started this attack, she has been fighting. She has been killing these creatures in the dozens. All around her are bodies of her foes. None being able to handle her toxins. Shaking her head at this assault.

"Well at least they aren't tough." She thought.

Opening her jaws, she grabs a dark hunter flying to her. Seeing more approaching her Emil gets ready. Flinging toxins at a rushing hunter. The toxins paralyze it then starts to dissolve it. Stomping on a skull of one.

One dark quill alpha rush towards her. Grappling with the berserker alpha. The alpha tries to claw her face. Emil moves it out of reach. Trying to grasp its head so she can crush it. It puts all its force in trying to overpower her. Taking a chance, she hurls it away causing the dark quill to hit the floor.

"Prepare to die pest." Emil says in mild irritation.

Breathing in she releases a beam upon it. The toxic beam burning straight through it. What is left start to disintegrate and fall apart. Not paying any mind of the fallen. Emil turns her head and fires another beam. Demolishing a group of hunters and alphas.

"You know. I am usually chill. But you guys are making me toxic." Emil says in an irritated tone.

"Oh well. The faster we exterminate you the faster I can relax." She states.

Vultures and death avians start to feed on unattended cadavers. Not absentmindedly though. They watch the battle closely. Just in case they need to flee.

You never know when a stray attack might hit you. Nothing wants to die out of nowhere. Plus, it is nice to see escape routes. Or more locations of food. This night will have left a bountiful feast.

Emil jumps back from the strike of the alpha. The dark quill attempts to impale her with its many legs. Hopping over the attack she gets behind it. Seeing it stumble to turn around she goes for the attack. Ripping out the dark koatl's spine.

Emil narrows her eyes as the corpse falls. Glancing at the spine in her she sighs. Dropping it to the ground. She coats her hands in toxins to get rid of the blood. Looking around she notices the carnage.

Continuing her investigation of the area something catches her attention. Maria's body laying in the distance. Emil's eyes widen from what she is witnessing.

"No. My poor apprentice is dead." She muttered remorseful. "You will be avenged."

Moving her gaze, she sees more battles taking place. Though she was focus on one specific fight. Emil moved her gaze to see Leon and Lily. And they were being badly beaten.

"You two hold on! I am coming!" She shouts.

Emil starts running to aid them. Multiple dark quills start to impede her. Slicing through many attackers who tried to stop her. Grabbing an alpha by the head. Then crushing it. Nothing was going to stop her.

Oliver fires off a shot from his mouth. The projectile tearing straight through the hunter. He turns to another and fires a gray beam. Eradicating the dark quill. He lets out a huff.

"Do these things ever stop coming?" Oliver questioned sarcastically.

He looks to a crowd of the heading his way. Releasing a sigh, he turns to them. Oliver plans to kills all of them before they could reach him.

"All right it is go time." He lets a smirk form on his face.

His body bulks up a bit. Two cannon shaped appendages emerge from his back. Fin like pieces on top of them. Then turret shaped flesh covered Oliver's arms. Raising his arms to his face.

He lets out a laugh. "Been awhile sense I could cut loose like this," He shakes his head. Oliver glances back to the rushing enemies. "Well, time to die!" He cackles as missiles fire from his back. Zooming the air, they crash down on the forces.

Blue blood splatters across the ground. Burnt limbs fly in the air. Right before crashing down. "How you like that," Aiming his arm guns. **Bang! Bang! Bang! Bang! Bang!** He fires with rapid speed.

Bodies fall one by one. Bullet holes filling their bodies. Oliver laughs at all the bodies he is catching. Aiming his cannons at another spot of the crowd. **Boom!** A pair of missiles hit dark quill alphas. Their forms being blasted apart.

"Oh. This is what I call fun." He states.

"Man., I wonder how the others are doing." He finishes.

Turning to face down more enemies. Oliver spots his targets. A group of hunters charge forward. A boulder belabors the leading one. After connecting it blows up. Killing the surrounding dark quills.

"Ilya, nice to see that you are joining in." He says with a smirk.

"Thought you needed some help." She commented.

"While not needed, it would be helpful." Oliver answers back.

"Oh whatever. Let's just get to killing." Ilya spoke. Then looks at him. "I see you are bringing the big guns out."

"I figured I could make this entertaining." Oliver said.

A squad of alphas approaches them with speed. Fangs and claws bared. Bloodlust in their eyes.

"Enough of this." Letting out a sigh. Oliver fires the cannons on his back. Blasting multiple dark quills to bits.

"I think I will follow your example." Ilya announced.

Massive fins erupt from her back and arms. Two on her back and one on each arm. Ilya flaps her fins and propels herself into the air. Hovering in the air her feet and tail morph into guns. A twisted grin appears on her face.

Ilya now ready to assist Oliver attacks. Aiming her guns, she fires. **Bang! Boom! Bang! Bang! Boom! Boom!** Explosions erupt throughout the area. Bullets slam into dark quills only to explode the following second. Oliver shoots trio of hunters. Making mincemeat out of them.

"I am perceiving now what you meant by fun." She remarks. "This is a fun way of doing this."

Flying up to meet her was a pair of uropygid alphas. Ilya scoffs at their attempt to harm her. Then proceeds to light them up. Blasts color the sky. Highlighting the slow sunrise. "Let's kick this up a notch!" She exclaims. Ilya starts spinning in the air and lets out bullets in multiple directions. Decimating dark quills.

Lily lets out a scream as a tentacle impales her shoulder. "Aah!" She is hoisted in the air then slammed into Leon. Wrapping a tendril around Leon's leg Ren throws him in the air. Then coils two tentacles in a shape of a club. Swinging them in the air, they collide with Leon smacking him into the ground. Ren glances at Lily. Yanking her to him to finish her off.

"Time to go ahead and finish you off." Ren informs her.

Lily quickly cuts off the tendril holding her. "Argh!" Before she could press her attack, she is grabbed. Grasping her head and arms with his bladed tentacles. Lily opens her mouth to release a beam. Only for the tendril holding head to tighten. Shutting her mouth.

"Now no need for that. Just embrace your death." He whispered in a monotone voice.

Tugging on her arms to secure his hold. Ren plunges his claws into her torso. Lily tries to release a scream, but it is muffled. Gripping her body with both hands he pulls them apart. Tearing her body in half. Blood freely spilling from her dying upper half. Ren stares at her half-lidded eyes. Coiling harder he crushes Lily's head killing her.

"One down, one to go." He spoke.

Turning to the recovering Leon. Tossing the corpse towards him. It makes contact knocking him to the ground. Ren starts walking towards him. Leon manages to stand up. "I will kill you for this," He growled at the dark quill leader.

"Not likely." Ren replies.

Tendrils rapidly approach Leon. Both of his legs are impaled by the kneecaps. Next his biceps were stabbed. "Aah! Aah!" He howls in anguish. Leon is then lifting into the air. Ren stares up at him.

"Time to join your friend beast." He says with a mild smirk amused by these creatures.

"Not yet, I won't. You will be coming with me!" Leon yells.

Firing his breath attack at the dark quill meso. Ren just counters with a beam of his own. A whitish beam with a black outline collides with an orange beam. Both seem to be able to hold out. Ren starts pulling at Leon's limbs.

This causes him to falter in beam attack. The pain making him lose focus. Ren's blast slices through Leon's and connects with his head. Bringing the beam down he slices his body in half. Retracking his tentacles from the bisected cadaver.

"Well, that was kind of fun. Guess I should go ahead and eat their corpses." Ren thought. *"I want to use these goliath abilities."*

Right before he could start feeding, he is accosted. Emil tackles the beast. Ren tries to seize her with two of his tentacles. She with haste slices through two of the tentacles. Grabbing the remaining two Emil swings the smaller creature around. With no remorse bangs him into the floor.

"How dare you kill those two!" She shrieked at him.

"Easy. They challenged me and I killed them." He says as his tendrils regenerate.

"Though, I will admit they were slightly challenging." He adds.

Emil is infuriated at what she just heard. He thinks of this as a game. Two of her students had died because of a game. She will show this beast that this is no game. A ball of different toxins forms in her hands.

She quickly hurls at the meso. The ball crashes into him takes effect. His left arm is melted off to the elbow. Then the secondary effect kicks in. Something that he notices.

"What the? Why is my regeneration slowing down. Also, I can't move my left side." Ren ponders in his head.

The toxic goliath doesn't give any more time to think. Emil crashes into him. Swiping her claws across his body. Leaving lacerations upon him. Within seconds disappear from his body. He swiftly kicks her off him.

And punches her in the leg. Emil stumbles back from the hit. Ren tries to coil his tentacles around her leg. Right as he does that Emil drips burning toxins on the limbs. Burning right them.

Ren recoils from this. Gritting his teeth in mild pain and annoyance. Emil fires a torrent of toxins at Ren. Rolling away he avoid the beam. However, he couldn't avoid the follow up attack.

Leaping forward Emil swipes her hand towards him. Flinging arcs of toxins slicing into him. All he could do was block with his tendrils. The trails connect with the tendrils. Burning and paralyzing them.

"What's wrong? You seemed so sure of yourself." Emil asked coldly.

Before he could respond she runs forward. Snatches him up before slamming him the ground. She rips off his tendrils. She proceeds to start slashing him. Removing one of his mandibles.

His reformed tendrils crash into her. Causing her to stumble back. Ren starts swinging at her. But that doesn't stop her. Forming club with her hand she smacks him back to the ground. Ren's back crashes back into the dirt.

"You don't get to escape. Only death." She states in a cold tone.

Stomping down on his chest. Pining him to the desert floor. He tries to struggle with all his might. It is for naught, however.

Emil opens her mouth and blasts him with a beam. Melting his flesh and paralyzing him in the process. Seeing that Ren can't move or regenerate currently she goes on the attack. Tearing off his arms piece by piece. Ripping out his chest along with his organs. Clamping down on his head with her jaws. With effort removes his head from his body. Emil crushes his head in her mouth. Spitting it out she then melts the whole body. Leaving nothing behind.

"I have avenged you little ones." Emil huffs out.

Turning her gaze, she witnesses as her allies slaughter the enemy. Without their leader many dark quills retreat from the area. Knowing they will not survive this encounter. Emil's eyes land back on Leon's corpse. She walks up and strokes his body.

In the distance Ivan is seen doing the same to Marie. A tear falling from his eye. Many lives were lost today. This will not go unanswered. They will be ready for the enemy the next time.

Epilogue

Viper and Mist stare at the remains of Hydra. Both let out a mournful sigh. Hydra was a good friend of theirs. It was little sad seeing him dead like this. Mist shakes her head at this outcome.

"Good by friend. See you in the afterlife." She muttered.

Her and Viper look up at the sound of flapping wings. Calamity has made his return. He looks to the two of them. They shake their heads. Viper points to the body of the ice dragon.

"He didn't make it. He was burnt to death." She said in monotone.

"I see. It's a shame him and the others died." He said with disappointment in his voice. "Viper can you use your venom to melt his body. I don't want any of the small races taking his parts." He added.

Viper nodded her as she moves closer to his body. Opening her mouth, a stream of venom drops onto Hydra's corpse. His body starts to dissolve into mush. When there isn't anything solid left she stops.

"It is done." She states.

"Well let's fly back to the mountain. To inform everyone of the situation." Calamity instructs them. "Also, to make them aware of potential rouge dragons in the area."

"Yes sir!" They both yell.

With the flap of their wings, they take off into the air. Their gazes linger on the dragon remains. Shifting their eyes, they take off. Their destination the large mountain. With grief in their hearts, they fly with purpose.

"Hope we won't lose anybody else." Mist hoped.

Oliver and Ilya stare down at the bodies of their teachers and teammates. Both, grief stricken. They couldn't understand how it came to this.

"Lily, River." Oliver said sadly.

"Calmar, Claire." Ilya added in sadness.

"At least you all went out fighting." He stated in content. "We will remember you all."

"We will also avenge you. These beasts will be hunted and slaughtered." She spoke with glowing eyes. Trembling in rage.

"Leon no! Waah! Waa! Why?! My brother why?!" Dawn bawling her eyes out.

Clutching his body in her arms. Tears dripping from her eyes. Splattering on him. Chloe rubs her shoulder to comfort her. She lets out a sad huff.

"Maria no." Helga mumbles to herself.

Maria's corpse held in her arms. Today she lost two friends. Them both to unidentified creatures. A tear drips down her cheek. Many goliaths are now taking in the aftermath.

Emil looks over to Oliver and Ilya. She makes her way to them. She approaches them. Both turn to look at her.

"I know this isn't what you would like to hear right now. But if it helps you both can join my group if you want." Emil tells them.

Both face each other and nod. Then they look back at her. "We are both fine with that." Oliver informs her. Emil nods and leaves them to their mourning. She has her own to do after all.

Whitespine walks through the corridors of one of their bases. Entering a room his stops. Looking around he sees many dark quills here. Many types and classes. Then he felt something.

"Hmm? What was that?" He pondered.

"Oh. Ren and Gray have died. Interesting." He mumbled. "Hope Ness is doing well on her journey. Either way new DNA and information has been learned." He adds.

"You all are ready to do your duty for the hive correct?" Whitespine says as he turns to the group of mesos in the room.

"Yes sir!" They shouted in confirmation.

It doesn't matter how long it will take. He will succeed in getting what he wants. No matter the obstacles. The dark quills will prevail. And this whole planet will learn. This will be his world.

Printed in the United States
by Baker & Taylor Publisher Services